I0724301

EXTER BARREN

NEWSHAWK

ADULT FICTION
based on actual events

Cub reporter to international journalist visiting over 100 countries, with romantic encounters and adventures told in first person

WORKBOOK PRESS LLC
187 E Warm Springs Rd,
Suite B285, Las Vegas, NV 89119, USA

Website:	https://workbookpress.com/
Hotline:	1-888-818-4856
Email:	admin@workbookpress.com

Ordering Information:
Quantity sales. Special discounts are available on quantity purchases by corporations, associations, and others.
For details, contact the publisher at the address above.

ISBN-13:	978-1-955459-29-7 (Paperback Version)
	978-1-955459-30-3 (Digital Version)

REV. DATE: 11/05/2021

Dexter Barren
NEWSHAWK

NEWSHAWK
SYPNOSIS

Dexter Barren's father is a former army Chapin who served in the Second World War. After the war he continued life as a missionary. His family of three sons and a daughter travel with him to several countries. Dexter, his second son is quick to learn languages, and become a very proficient linguist.

This story is told in the first person and starts in Dexter Barren's childhood though to his teenage and continues onward to his adulthood. He makes a choice of career from three alternatives. The Church, Professional football or journalism. He chooses the later.

Attended his older brother's wedding before he marries his own teenage sweetheart an Anglo Filipino when he is 17 in a join wedding with his sister. Dexter has two children son, Aqyza, destined to following in his father's footsteps as a journalist and the daughter Linda who realized her ambition to be an actress.

Being a News Correspondent visits several countries. Women find him ultra-attractive and have designs on his body and his lack of self- control is exposed.

Locations in the UK include Colchester. Halstead, and Hempstead all in Essex. Borehamwood, Elstree om Hertfordshire and parts of North London, Bournemouth, Devon, Manchester and Leeds. In Scotland; Bathgate Glasgow, Inverness and Wick, Overseas in Ghana, South

Africa, The Congo, India, Columbia, Canada, USA, The Philippines Etc.

He has two mistresses.

The Scottish actress Penny he met on a snowbound train and becomes a family friend and helps his daughter Linda in her acting career. Later, Penny marries him after the shocking death of his wife Yvonne.

The Indian Lady, Usher born in the UK he met on her way to marry her 80-year-old fiancé in and arranged marriage. The marriage is without love and after her husband dies becomes a rich woman and returns to the UK to start her own boutiques.

Whilst doing his National service in the RAF is a reluctant advocate for a man who has gouged the face of a soldier. Rescues a squire from robbers, saves a man's life when he has a heart attack in his tractor. Almost killed by a sniper in Angola, kills a man in Africa, observes carnage in India, a shooting in Glasgow, kidnapped in Columbia, plus many more exciting incidents to enthrall you, including many erotic sexual encounters.

There is a unique twist in this novel, so you are advised to read it from start to finish to fully appreciate the impact that will continue to mesmerize you long after you have finished reading it.

CONTENTS

Chapter 1

MY EARLY MEMORIES

My name is Dexter Barren and I have decided to tell my story, most of it is interesting but there are obviously some dull sections that I will skip; so your continued reading will not be boring.

How far I go back in my life is dependent upon my memory. This life story is a mostly based on fact. Most destinations remain the same in most instances, but names have been changed to protect the culprits and the innocent.

My first memory was of as a child being evacuated to my Grandfather's farm in Essex after my birth in London. My mother was there with me whilst my father a Chaplin in the RAF was overseas in the desert. We were travelling on the local omnibus into Colchester and I was only 2 years of age and a curiosity about money. My little hands went into the money bag of the bus conductor and I withdrew 2 half-crowns without the conductor knowing. I raised the money in my hands and said to my mother "look mummy money, money" My mother instantly realized that I had taken this from the conductors bag and apologised for my light-fingered escapade. Maybe I was destined to become a pickpocket. However my parents were not poor and so a vision of being an Oliver Twist never materialized. My second memory was of being in the family home in London. My father was back from the war and I was 4 years of age give and take a few months weeks and days. The hosepipe was fixed onto the tap in the kitchen as the gardener was giving the garden a watering, I must have been strong for a young baby as I pulled the hose off the pipe and the entire kitchen was flooded. Not me to get the blame but the poor gardener was sacked instantly for being incompetent. I was less than forthcoming with the truth as the gardener left complaining that he had fixed the hosepipe properly. Visions of me perhaps becoming a strongman in a circus could have possible been envisaged.

I move forward to the day I started infant school and being taken by my nanny to the infant class. I was not in a good mood having been woken from my sleep and brutally hauled along to an alien environment with kids I did not know. My reaction as I saw my Nanny walk away was to punch as innocent child on the nose. Maybe I was cut out to be a pugilist, I was remonstrated with, in respect of my outburst, but later my victim and I were to become great friends, Godfrey and I were to share the same career. Both entered the RAF as officers and we both became journalists in our own right. We also shared a love of drama and sport. We still joke about the time I punched his nose. What away to strike up a friendship, however I don't recommend this to any of my readers who might find that they would force a reaction from whoever they hit to respond and give them a bloody nose, perhaps even more than they had bargained for.

As I stated before my father was an Army Chaplin during the WW2, so my early years after my birth I was not seeing much of him. The war over and being just 6 years old the family moved to Germany in 1946 that's my two brothers, Derek the oldest and Dean the youngest and our older sister

Denise. My mother Doreen and Father Desmond. Father became a missionary for 10 years after the war and retired at 55. My mother a farmer's daughter and during the war we were evacuated to his farm in Essex. I was quick to learn the German language and by the time we left Germany after 1 year, I was quite fluent in that language and French. We then got posted as a family to Barcelona. Mum, Dad my two brothers and my sister. Derek my older brother was five years my senior (half-brother from my father's first marriage, his mother died from cancer when he was 18months old). In Spain once more my linguistic talents helped me to learn Spanish, Portuguese and Italian. We stayed in Spain for 10 months before we came back to England to spend 3 years in The Philippines where I soon learned the native tongue, Tagalong and to speak Chinese (but not to write).

I was 13 when I returned to Britain and lived with my grandparents as Dad and Mum went to Ghana for 3 years. My father finally returned home to semi-retirement acting in a capacity of a lay preacher meaning he preached in several Churches in the UK, I visited him several times whilst he was in Ghana.

My parents sent me to a private school in Buckinghamshire St Columbus to continue my education I found the pleasure of treading the boards a real delight. I was in six dramas three musicals and three pantomimes during my stay at this public school. My nickname I was given was Weevil. I suppose because like the Weevil I was into everything, Sub editor of the school magazine, playing cricket, football, acting etc.

I did unfortunately attract the attention of a couple of bullies. Who tried to deprive me of my satchel and various private items? I did manage to avoid them most of the time but they did rob me of my soccer boots and diary. They also used to prevent me from entering into the common room. I did not want an argument so I walked away. I did bide my time and when one of the bullies was confined to bed with food poisoning. Should have been both of them but the other one did not eat his porridge. I can own up now I put a concoction into his food to get my own back. Whilst the other bully was on his own and tried to taunt me I turned on him with anger (the bitten bites back) I was pushing his head against the wall. As I did so my eyes were closed so I could not see the blood pouring of his head. No teachers were in the vicinity but when a shout from the watching crowd of boys was made very loudly. I opened my eyes and let his limp body fall to the ground. No prosecution was taken against me, as nobody would admit to seeing the incident. My former assailant to his credit did not reveal my name. In our school telling tales was strictly taboo. If anybody broke this unwritten rule, woe betide him, as his fate would have been horrendous, I won't go into too many details but to say that one boy caught telling tales was hung from a tree by his feet. Totally naked and covered in black tar. He was not rescued until a house master heard his cries some time later after his ridicule had been put into operation.

I excelled in geography and English and won top honours to enable me to go onto university. I declined this chance and persuaded my father that I wanted to be a journalist. Despite his misgivings I was not to follow in his desired profession for me as a Chaplin he gave his blessing for me to work on the local newspaper The Essex Rural Echo.

As a 16 year old I was fortunate to be able to perform well as a cub reporter the youngest they had ever employed. On the Echo I remember well my first visit to the local court where a middle-aged man was up before the magistrates for incident exposure and urinating against a church wall. The only witness was a teenage lady who claimed he was masturbating against the wall. As the case went on, I believed he was innocent from my original position of thought he was guilty. I was there to write the facts not put my opinion. Despite the defendant claiming that the nearby toilets were closed he had the desire to urgently spend a penny. Despite a character witness being called and giving a creditable of testimony of his character the magistrate wasted no more than a few seconds consulting with the other two magistrates on the bench both women. He declared he was guilty as charged and ordered a custodial sentence of 3 months.

A few days later the case came up on appeal to the crown court and I attended to write down the facts. The defence lawyer asked the only witness the teenage girl "What is your job Miss Smith" She paused "Um. Not employed" she replied. The lawyer shook his head "You know what is a lie" Miss Smith you work as a prostitute and you have been charged more than once of soliciting, trading your body for money" Miss Smith's face turned red. She had no alternative but to admit that was her profession. The judged deemed but her evidence as suspect and halted the proceeding and said "what you saw, was not what you said you saw him doing, he was in fact shaking his member to clear off the residue of urinal fluid from the end of his member so he would not wet his pants when he returned it inside of his flies. The man was found not guilty and the judge considered that the defendant had served sufficient sentence for exposure and not committing a lewd act, which was what the original charge related to. There were many other cases I reported on at the magistrate's court but non as colourful as the man who urinated against the church wall.

I continued with the Rural Echo until I was 20 and had several interviews with national papers. However, 3 of them offered me a job but the terms and conditions were not suitable, all they wanted was a glorified tea boy. My big break came a week after my 20th birthday an Australian News agency contacted me and invited me to be their correspondent in London. This was too god an opportunity to pass up. I accepted post after an interview held at the Australian Embassy in London at double my present salary and financial help for a flat in London.

Flashback to my recreational time whilst in Essex, you will find this to be a romantic episode in my life and experiencing my first experience of carnal knowledge.

I had just finished my stint at the court and as I was walking towards the bus stop when a car mounted the pavement and it was just a few feet away from striking the lady Slim taller than my 5ft 8 by at least 4 inches long dark hair and blue piercing eyes. I quickly pushed her against the wall and the car sped off.

The girl was horizontal on the pavement shaken but not hurt. I helped her to her feet. She smiled "You saved my life" She threw her arms round me and showered kisses around my lips and head. It all happened so fast people were standing and clapping for my heroics. The car had obviously been forced to mount the pavement as a flat truck lorry was rumbling down the road out of control minus the driver. I was caught up in the hoard of people running down the road to see the lorry plough through the plate glass front window of the fish and chip shop injuring a number of customers. My camera was out and taking a few photos and trying to interview a few of the bystanders. All this time the lady her name I found out later was Carol Carson the lady I rescued from the car mounting the pavement, was hanging on to me.

Shortly after concluding taking witness notes from the sixth bystander, Carol gently took my arm and propelled me away from the incident and then down a back alley, new pulling me along with a tight grip on my hand and up an iron exterior staircase and to a doorway that led into her flat. She pushed me onto the large red sofa, and her lips found mine she needed no invitation to deprive me of my clothes tie first then shirt and pulled my trousers off with my underpants and shoes too. Leaving me totally naked apart from my blue socks. She rapidly rid herself of her clothes to lay fully naked onto my torso. I was connected to her body by my appendage, the rest you can guess. We sat on the sofa after the deed and together we smoke a cigarette. She did not ask if I had enjoyed the copulation but told me her age was 28 and her name, and asked for mine. She was a little taken aback when I sold her I was only 16, Oh my God! She exclaimed, "so I must be your first fuck" I remembered nodding my head as I covered my now exhausted member with my shirt, whilst she brazenly still remains naked. She was impatient for further action and I for one felt powerless to resist as she sat astride me and gyrating her hips onto my pubes. All caution to the wind as I buried my mouth onto her ample proportions as they lay on my face. She was a lady of few words but at least declared in loud overtones "Dexter you are the best fuck I have ever had" She continued "I thought you were older than 16 younger than me of course but more likely early 20's" She paused "I normally go for guys in their 30's but you are half their age and more virulent than they are, that's not to say I have had a heap of guys just 12 since my first date at school when I was 14" She had lifted herself off me by now and gently kissing my lips again continued "That's only one a year is that bad or is it not bad" she chucked. "I do not know I never been with a woman before" I paused "well not for full sex just fooling around" She stroked my face with the back of her hand "Tell me dear Dexter, "how many girls have you as you say, fooled around with" 6 but only 2 of them just kissing and the other 4 we only touched groped each other in intimate parts." Carol laughed as she pulled herself up from the sofa and walked naked into kitchen. "I am going to make us something to eat and drink what would you like tea coffee or something stronger, and his ham eggs and chips OK for you. "Coffee and yes the food is OK, I love ham and eggs" I responded.

We talked a little as we ate by this time we had both dressed, albeit me in underpants and shirt whilst she wore a crimson silk see through negligee. That did little to cover her delicious body. I was in love at that time but later to realize it was infatuations being the first time I had fornicated.

The Chronicle newspaper our rival paper in Colchester carried a photo of the lorry in the front of the chip shop and myself albeit only my back braced against the wall with carol under the headline unidentified man pushes lady to safety. Of course they knew it was me but being a rival newspaper did not want to afford publicity to the Echo my own newspaper carried my full report on the incident including a few lines in which I stated I had pushed a lady out of the way of a car that mounted the pavement.

I continued to see Carol for a further 6 weeks but we were never seen out together. She was quite adamant that she had a reputation to maintain and being seen with a guy almost half her age would invite sarcastic comments. I was happy to play along with this as the sex between us was getting better and better. I was becoming obsessed with her and although we only met twice a week, Monday and Wednesday I did spend the nights in her bed, telling my parents I was staying with a friend which was not exactly a lie.

Carol was a northern girl having lived most of her life in Leeds and came to Colchester to work for a branch of the bank she was employed by. What she never told me for 6 weeks was that her secondment to Colchester was only for 1 year and that in a few days' time she would be going back to Leeds. I was heartbroken but she promised to write and sometime invite me to stay in Leeds. I had to admit that my heart was very heavy and tears formed in my eyes as I kissed her goodbye at the station. I did notice that there seemed to be no emotion on her face for her separation from me. She never did write, and it took me awhile to get over our short clandestine but very intimate relationship.

Chapter 2

I COULD SMELL THE FRAGRANCE OF HER PERFUME

Three months later I met a girl a month younger than myself. I saw her standing at the bus stop in Colchester. I made my way in her direction to catch my bus back to Halstead. She was standing on her own her arm in bandage and laid in a sling. I plucked up courage to ask her "what happened to your arm" "I fell down some stairs at work" she informed me just as the bus rolled up. We sat on the bus next to each other and got better acquainted. Yvonne was her name and only a month younger than myself. The oriental look to her facial features prompted me to ask her in Tagalog *Ikaw galing Phils* meaning, are you from the Philippines. She looked surprised but answered me in Tagalog. *Ang aking nanay ay mula sa Philippines* meaning her mother was from the Philippines. I explained "I spent 3 years in The Philippines in Davao and Manila with my father a missionary and visited many cities there", I paused "would you prefer I speak Tagalog or English?" Yvonne smiled, "Please speak English as my knowledge of my Mother's tongue is limited, and you probably speak better than I do, as I have never been to The Philippines, I was born in Colchester."

The bus journey back to Halstead took just over 40 minutes and in that time we got on so well that as we got off the bus I asked her "Do you have a boyfriend Yvonne?" No she replied "Do you have a girlfriend?" No! I answered "Would you think me too forward if I asked you out for a date perhaps to go to the Empire cinema in Halstead to see 'The King and I' starring Yul Brynner and Deborah Carr." Yvonne smiled and replied. "Yes please Dexter, I would love to see that film, thank you".

Yvonne lived on the Sudbury Road with her parents, her

Father George and Englishman who owned a bakery in Castle Hedingham and delivered bread and cakes to many local shops in Haverhill, Braintee, Halstead, Hedingham, Yeldham and Ridgewell etc. Her mother Connie was born in The Philippines in General Santos City and her Father met her there when he was stationed there during the war attached to an American unit. He got married to her there and before the Japanese invaded the islands, they came to the UK Her mother was already pregnant with Yvonne and gave birth to her in early January 1940 a month after I was born.

That evening Yvonne and myself went to The Empire to see the film. We had to queue for 20 minutes and we made more congenial conversation. Finding out more about her past history and relationships with her parents. In the cinema we were allocated seats in the middle of the auditorium. We watched the film in silence and I plucked up courage to put my arm round her and she snuggled up close to me so I could smell the fragrance of her perfume. At 5ft, she was 8 inches shorter than me. Long black hair a slim figure and small breasts and a slightly dark skin, invitingly brown eyes, a pert nose, than lips and when she smiled she displayed her pure white straight teeth. Although her face was close to mine I resisted the temptation to kiss her until I felt she would be happy to reciprocate. After all we had only met a few hours before and the last thing I wanted to do was for her to loose respect for me, as I was the first boy to take her out on a date.

Our second date and I was invited to meet her parents. I dressed formally in a clean white shirt, tie and dark trousers and a light jacket. Not wanting to be too hot as the summer evening was very close and humid. I knocked on the door of Yvonne's parents home and was greeted by her father George who open the door to me. He greeted me in the Tagalog language and I responded likewise. Reverting to English he praised me "You speak the language of the Phils very fluently, but we speak English here in our home as I don't speak the language too good and Yvonne as you know was born here so her first tongue is English". Meeting Connie, I greeted her in Tagalog and she responded also in her native tongue before we again spoke in English.

I sensed straight off that her parents warmed to me and when they found out my Father was a preacher, they were both impressed. They went to the same church as I did, but as so many people crammed into the church at the top of the High Street, getting to know everybody was a mammoth task at the best of times. Most Sundays over 300 people attended this church and on holy days this would advance to well over 500 or more persons, some forced to stand or go to one of the other churches in the town.

On the Sunday, I went with my parents' sister and younger brother to the church in our Sunday best. After all it was fitting that with my father leading the service at the church this particular Sunday his family should be well turned out for the occasion. I met and introduced Yvonne and her family to my family and we sat together in the pews minus my father of course who was leading the service. After the service Yvonne accepted my parents' invitation to have dinner at my parent's home so they could become better acquainted. All of a sudden in a matter of days It seemed this was to be a serious relationship.

My mother offered to cut up Yvonne's dinner seeing as she had her arm in a bandage and sling. No "Mrs. Barren its ok I can still use my hand but I keep it in a sling on Doctors' advice when I can" She explained. My Brother Dean always the curious one and with his mouth almost full of food asked indignantly "How long you known my brother," before should answer he posed a very personal question "Is he good at kissing?" At that point my Father reprimanded him in a raised voice "Dean, you do not ask our guests such personal question, button it or go to your room". There was a pregnant pause before my father continued offering apologies to Yvonne for Deans obvious intrusion into her personal space.

It was a traditional Sunday English roast with all the trimmings followed by spotted dick (Suet puddling with currants) and lashing of homemade custard. We made congenial but non-intrusive conversation throughout the meal. My father remembered some of his Tagalog and spoke a few of the more common place words which she understood admitting that her knowledge of the language was not fluent only little that she had learnt from her mother.

Mother declined Yvonne's offer of help with the washing up declaring that my brother Dean and Sister Denise would assist her. She bade us both to go for a walk. "Make the most of this hot sunny weather as it's not often June is as hot as this", Yvonne thanked my mother and Father for their hospitality. I put on my jacket but once outside in the full glare of the sun I laid it over my shoulder, Yvonne was dressed in a light cotton flower dress down below her knees but with bare shoulders and revealing a demure glimpse of her cleavage with just a crimson belt to hold it in, so as to show that her waist was slim neat black flat shoes and white socks her hair long but whilst in a church and at my parent home wore it in a ponytail. She let her hair down as we walked hand in hand down the footpath that lead to the river. We past a few older youths and they made comments about being with a nigger. I could have reacted but I remembered the last time I had been in a fight in the Philippines, when two Philippine boys started throwing stones at Derek Dean and myself. We did react and after a few clenched fists mostly from Derek Dean and myself we put the boys on their backs with bloodied noses and bleeding torsos mostly from the rough terrain, as Derek lay into them with his heavy black boots.

When Father found out about this he called us into the study. "I hear what you did today to 3 young boys throwing stones at you, you should have walked away as this is no way for the sons of a missionary to behave" He removed his thick heavy belt from his trousers. We were in for a thrashing and the first and last time our father ever gave us other than with his hands against our naked legs on a few occasions maybe 4 or 5 times. We bent down in front of him ready to take our punishment, the eldest first and on our naked buttocks, he delivered 2 strokes for each of us. We were not able to sit down with comfort for a few hours. With this in mind, I showed restraint and explained that it was not fitting for a Christian to retaliate. I was grateful they did not follow us with further racist comments or the temptation to lash out would have been difficult to be restrained. Both my brothers and myself had been taught the art of self-defence in Judo and similar arts that also include boxing. Father pointed out having the ability to use these arts would often deter assailants, but kicking out at the stone throwers as we did in the Philippines was a definite no go activity.

We reached the river and were surprised at the absence of other people in the immediate vicinity. We had walked quite some way along the riverbank whereas most people were gathered close to the pathway to the main road. We lay down on the grass and Yvonne took a blade of grass and gently stroked my face with it, before bringing her face close to mine, so close that I could feel her breath upon my cheeks. She pursed her lips. This was the invitation I had desired and knowing she would not repel my lips on hers. Our mouths I held her head as I rolled over to be astride her my torso against hers. Yes, feeling and eruption of sorts in my trouser. This was not the time to devour her virginity. Kissing only and it must have lasted for all of 5 minutes and how we learned to breathe gently through our noses to keep this fusion of our lips together.

I held her left hand gently squeezing it as we walked back from our romantic rendezvous. She had now removed her right hand from the sling and gently held it across her chest. There were many kisses to follow as we walked back pausing several times to exchange our passion of love. We talked about a future and when later that week she would go back to her doctor to see if she could take the bandage off.

If it was infatuation with Carol, with Yvonne it was love. This is what I felt for she wanted to be with me. No hiding me away from public view as Carol had demanded. As we were walking up to the door of her house she whispered in my ear *Mahal kita* Dexter. I responded in English, I love you too Yvonne. I enjoyed an interesting conversation with her family and we laughed about many interesting tales that we related about the Philippines.

Later that week, Yvonne had her bandage removed and for the first time, I was able to see both of her arms in their true beauty. During the next three weeks of the month of June, we made many trips to the riverside and although I got many peculiar looks from local people when I was with Yvonne, I did not let it disturb me.

Chapter 3

WE GOT US A MURDER HERE

There were no other Asian people or any Africans in Halsted or the nearby villages. To some people seeing people of a different colour or culture was something they could not come to terms with. In Colchester and Chelmsford the big cities in Essex a number of Caribbean immigrants were arriving and there was a feeling of discrimination in evidence. Maybe the local white Anglo Saxons were afraid of them. In Colchester where I worked some people would cross the road to avoid them and in the public houses so I was told some pulicans refused to serve them. They were there though to do the jobs that the white people were reluctant to do. They were in the 50's considered to be a lower class of humanity. This I did not subscribe to since in God's eyes we are all the same. In the Colchester churches the immigrants in general were well-received and very little animosity. In the streets however the term nigger and jungle bunny were to be often repeated.

When I was with Yvonne and we were holding hands in public, I was often called a nigger lover, I chose to ignore such insidious comments. However, it was on one occasion that whilst in the town and Yvonne and I were looking through the glass of a local shop that a local boy older then I shoved us both against the window and started to punch me in the chest and face, I had to defend myself and with one blow to his head, I laid him out cold on the pavement and taking Yvonne's hand we left the scene of the incident, and took her to her own home.

When I arrived at my home, I was greeted by my Father who told me that the police wanted to interview me in respect of my attack on a boy in the Town. There were two witnesses who had lied to the police that I had without any provocation attacked the named individual. In consequence, I was charged with causing actual bodily harm. My father believed to me be innocent in respect of the charge and we employed the services of a local solicitor to defend me in the local magistrates court a few days later. The defence had located 4 people who had seen the incident and supported my claim that I was provoked and only defended myself in retaliation to being hit by the assailant. The prosecution called the 2 witnesses and both their statements were in question as there were several discrepancies. The prosecution were bemused when the 4 witnesses found by my solicitor all supported my claim of defending myself. Two of the persons who had seen the incident from my defence were from the local church and the others just ordinary people who wanted to see justice in this case. The Magistrates took just less than a minute to dismiss the charge against me. The police then had no alternative but to bring charges against the youth who had attacked me with the additional charge of wasting police time and the two witnesses for him were also charged with perverting the course of justice by giving false evidence.

Six weeks into my relationship with Yvonne, and we did behave ourselves, much kissing of course, but beyond that was only to be in our imaginations. George and Connie asked me to stay overnight at their home to be with Yvonne at for one night whilst they visited friends in London from Saturday morning until Sunday afternoon. "We have our utmost respect for you Dexter and with this mind we would like you to stay overnight in our spare room so that Yvonne will not feel neglected, as this is the first time we have ever left her on her own" explained George. "We know she will be safe with you since you have over the last 2 months always shown a degree of sense and respect so I have no hesitation in asking you look after our little girl whilst we are away, and know you will not take liberties and respect our trust in you" Connie interjected. I interrupted, "Yvonne can always stay at my parents house, I can always share with my brother Dean for one night, she can have my room" George smiled and responded to my suggestion "No need Dexter, it will be more convenient for you to stay at our house less disturbance in your household with 6 of you there, no disrespect to you or your parents but I feel Yvonne would be more comfortable staying in her own home and bed.

We went to the Halstead Railway station to see her parents off and then returned to her house where she made me a snack of ham in two crusty rolls and tea of course. The rest of the day with the sun shining as full strength we took ourselves down to the riverside by far our favourite place to be. The water looked so inviting and with no person in the immediate vicinity I wanted to take a swim so suggested to Yvonne that we take the plunge. "We don't have our bathers Dexter, shall we go back and get them" I rubbed my chin and thought for a few seconds. "We can always go in with our underwear if that's OK with you." I suggested. Yvonne smiled looked back along the riverbank and content that nobody was in our immediate sight replied "OK! We can do that and dry ourselves in the sun."

This was the first time we had seen each other in our underwear, me in my Y fronts and she in her white bra and matching panties. I was transfixed at the beauty of her partially naked body with my mind working overtime at how she would look without anything on. She too was admiring my physique before we holding hands entered the clear blue water of the River Colne. As we moved towards the centre of the river it got deeper and we were both able to swim. This section of the river was quite wide about 15 feet I guessed from bank to bank. The water was warm and very much invigorating. We swam for about 10 minutes before we laid ourselves on the grass to soak up the sun for the intended drying of our bodies. Without a word spoken, I took the initiative to lay my hand upon her stomach and traced fingers upwards towards her breast and she gently took my hand and laid it upon her bra covered breast and I felt her left nipple beneath it. It was hard and was tempted to go under the bra but at that time just satisfied and a little nervous just to do what I was doing and moved my hand to her right breast and felt the nipple also hard under her bra cup. Her hand had now been placed on my inner thigh and gently moving upwards to rest upon my bulge and I could feel my member enlarging under my Y fronts by this show of intimacy. How far this familiarity would have led to was abruptly interrupted by the voices of children coming in our direction. We hastily pulled out clothes over our bodies as the children came past us just giving a casual glance before disappearing into the undergrowth and re-emerging to climb up onto the parapet of the road bridge. After a short period, we dressed and proceeded back to Yvonne's house with my imagination on overtime dreaming of what could have been but for the interruption by the children.

We spent the evening window-shopping in Halstead High Street. We admired some of the new gadgets on display in the windows, painfully aware that most of these electrical items were beyond the means of our paltry salaries. I was on just over £25 per month whilst Yvonne working in a Solicitors office hardly managed £15.00 a month. Most of the electrical items we admired would cost us our joint monthly salaries.

It was nice to see a few Americans in Town from the nearby RAF Wethersfield, who had just arrived in Britain part of a larger contingent to be based in the UK. For many people it was the first time they had seen black GI's in the town although I was to learn that there were a few visiting the town from the Nearby Ridgewell, Earls Colne and Gosfield aerodromes. During the war many local girls married American GI's black and white. Others had lost their virginity to them and lost their love as this indiscretion was reason to post them back to the States. Most never did hear of them again and were forced to bring the offspring up on their own with no support from the American Father.

We returned to Yvonne's home when darkness descended and watched TV. We had choice of only 2 channels then BBC and ITV all in black and white on an 8inch screen. Game shows like Hughie Green's *'double your money'* and Michael Miles *'Take your pick'* Hughie also hosted *'Opportunity Knocks'* a talent show. *'Sunday Night at the palladium'* hosted by Tommy Trinder. It was the show most people watched on a Sunday night with such stars as Bing Crosby, Norman Vaughn Petula Clark Bob Cummings, Naming but a few.

Yvonne turned the TV and waited a few minutes for it to warm up and then waited for the show Opportunity Knocks to start. We watched the array of talent some which we saw as doomed never to see the light of day whilst other we saw were later to become household names like Mary Hopkins Bonnie Langford Les Dawson Maureen Myers, Barry Cummings etc.

Having nestled on the sofa Yvonne's head on my lap and kissing her delightful lips when the adverts came on. We reflected that this was the first time we had been on our own in a house since we met a little over 2 months previous. We were free to do what we wanted and having been tempted down by the riverbank did we dare to take our relationship to new heights. There was temptation for the ultimate; that was only expected from married couples.

It was after 11 pm when we went to bed. At the doorway to Yvonne's bedroom we paused and kissed. There was a strong feeling that what I desired, she desired also. I wanted to be certain that she was as willing as I was I undressed to my birthday suit and slipped into bed. I only needed a sheet as my covering as the night was so humid. I was thinking of Yvonne and a few times I called out to her words such as "I love you darling" "I will dream of you" "I want you more than any other girl on this earth" etc.

Slowly I was slipping into dreamland. Was it a reality that I saw Yvonne standing by the door and lifting off her nightdress in the half-light produced by the full moon shining through the window! I was aware of her pulling back the sheet off my body to reveal my body as she had never seen it before and yes my member reacted to her presence. She laid her finger on my lips and whispered "Dexter it is time for us to show how much we mean to each other". I felt her naked body against mine her breathe; panting with excitement or nervousness. I could feel her heart beating so fast and my own heart pounding like a tank hurtling across the desert in anticipation of a confrontation.

The night was spent in each other's arms; we came close to total intercourse, but we both ensured that we maintained self-control. Not that we did not enjoy ourselves, as foreplay lasted a long time as we explored each other's body. Our bodies were still interlocked as we awoke that morning a little after 6 am. Both of us reluctant to separate our bodies from each other. We kissed so much and not just on the lips as we again explored each other's torso, even those parts hidden from public view. We gave ourselves to each other without shyness or inhibition. Out of the bed at half past 8, neither of us felt guilty for we had taken our love a step further but not into the realms of the ultimate purpose. It would come one day but to go too far too soon would not be in our mutual interest. We both realized that if we did, we would run the risk of being young parents and that was not what we wanted. We knew little about contraception only that restraint was the only form of contraception that we were are of at that time. I shuddered to think of the consequences if indeed we had copulated and she became pregnant. What would our parents think; in particular, the trust of her parents given to me to look after their little girl. The last thing I wanted was for me to be alienated from the girl I loved; it would break my heart for I dearly loved her with all my heart, soul and body.

After breakfast, we dressed in our Sunday best and walked to church arm in arm. My father greeted us with my mother and made a general enquiry of how we spent the evening. We told all but obviously left out the night of passion. It's just then that I suddenly remembered that the condition of the bed we both slept in. There were marks on the sheet that could be noticed, and that her bed would look as if nobody had slept in it. I whispered these thought to Yvonne in Church and she assured me that all tell-tale marks on the sheets had been eradicated whilst I went for a long soak in the bath she had washed out all the signs and marks on both the upper and lower sheets and disposed of the tissues that we put in the basket by the bed.

An invitation for lunch at my parents' home had already been agreed before Yvonne's parents went away. Our entire family were there including my older brother Derek his fiancé Rosemary soon to be his wife. A sweet demure lady 5ft 6 slim with long blonde hair and the age of 21 the same age as Derek, she older by one month only. They had met at university where she was also training to be a doctor. She had a healthy appetite for out Mother's food and very talkative. Later after lunch, Yvonne was in conversation with my soon to be sister-in-law whilst my two brothers and myself took ourselves out into the garden for a family conference with our father. My sister Denise was talking with my mother whilst they proceeded with the washing up.

The afternoon we spent as usual down by the riverside at our favourite place although we took our bathers, we took the plunge after due consideration and checking that we were alone to swim in our own skins. As we lay on the bank side, we talked a little and it was then that Yvonne had with due caution asked Rosemary about contraceptives. She had given her the advice we both required for when we did decide to take the ultimate step. We dressed and proceeded back to the town and without going to either of our homes walked down the hill to the station to meet her parents off the train. As we walked up the hill to their home, we talk about what we had done and about their day visiting old friends in Elstree and their tour of the film studious. They never pressed us for too many details about our day, but we volunteered only what we thought they would like to hear.

On Monday Morning, both Yvonne and myself caught the same bus into Colchester where both worked. It was not often that we both started work at the same time, but on this particular week I was on the middle shift 9 to 5 and would also be coming back on the same bus. We agreed to meet for lunch at the Tea house just off the High street. We talked a little about our morning activities, and our plans for the evening. We would catch a later bus and go to one of the cinemas in Cholchester, and have a meal at this fish and chip shop before we queued up to see a film.

We left the cinema at just after 10 pm having got in the first house and sat at the back of the auditorium where yes we held hands and kissed a lot. The journey home was uneventful and I walked her home before going back towards the town to go to my own home less than a mile away.

As I reached the junction of the Sudbury Road and Hedingham road I saw my Brother Derek and soon to be my sister-in-law coming up the hill so decided to wait for them. The saw me standing outside the men's outfitters and both waved at me. I crossed the road walked towards them. We had hardly come to facfe when we noticed a disturbance outside The White hard hotel. Four men were beating on an older man with large sticks. Derek asked Rosemary to sit on the bench as he and I crossed the road Derek issuing a waning "leave him alone you bullies" If I had not mentioned before my brother Derek was 6ft 3 and like myself we had both been tutored in the art of martial arts. Two of the bullies walked towards us banishing their sticks at head height. Their chance of using them was soon deprived as a swift kick to the pelvis by both of us to each of the bullies laid them out cold. Derek picked both bodies up and dragged them into the shop front of the gent's outfitters the two other guys wisely decided to make a run for it. Derek's priority was to attend to the victim and I assisted. We heard the police bell and the Black Maria soon drew up alongside us and two burly police officers raced over to where we were and raised their truncheons. "OK you are both under arrest" the Sergeant shouted out. The victim knowing the situation called out rather weakly. "These two boys came to my rescue they did not attack me" So where are the attackers now" ask the sergeant. Derek pointed in the direction of the shop. The constable walked over and noticed that they were both perfectly still. Sarge! He caked out "I think they are both dead looks like we got us a murder here. Derek and I stood motionless. Rosemary over to the 2 bodies and after prodding them they both started to regain consciousness. "What the hell did you do to them" the sergeant asked. Derek explained our martial arts experience. "Well, you two lads have probably saved this man from a more serious injury, maybe his life" The sergeant paused, and speaking to the victim continued" You will go to hospital soon an ambulance is on its way. A second police car was summoned and we including Rosemary were taken to the Halstead Police station where all 3 of us gave evidence. We had of course phoned our father from the station and he duly turned up and praised us for our good deed. IT was after midnight when we got home. I decided there and then once I got home to write out as much details as I could remember to take to the Echo in the morning.

The sergeant knocked on the door of our home at 6 45 am asking to see either my brother or myself. Still in our nightclothes plus dressing gowns we both went into the lounge and the officer informed us. "The victim was George Federer and he is OK and released from hospital after treatment. My father who was in the room exclaimed "Is that the George Federer who is the Squire over at Gestingthorpe?" "Yes the very same, and he wants to thank you boys personally, and asked med to ask you to telephone him ASAP so he can meet with you at his farm house". The sergeant concluded before he took his leave from our home.

Chapter 4

100 POUNDS EACH

When I went to Yvonne's home I was full of enthusiasm and arrived there earlier that I had stated, when we parted that previous night, Connie open the door "Why Dexter you are here so early Yvonne told me you would be here at 8 not 7 30" I have something to share with you all before we go to work. I explained. Both George, Connie and Yvonne listen to my account of the night's incident with awe and praise for the actions of both Derek and myself. I accepted a cup of tea from her parents and at 8 o'clock we walked down the hill to catch the bus. I must have bored Yvonne to tears as I could not stop repeating the activity of last night. Bless her heart she listened intently without complaint as over and over I repeated the same story. The only variation was more emphasis on what I had left out.

I had compiled the report on the incident and it read as this: Our local cub Reporter Dexter Barren and his older brother Derek came to the rescue of Squire Federer of Gestingthorpe late on Monday night when he was being attacked by four local villains in Halstead in Halstead town centre. Both Dexter and Derek were tutored in martial arts and using this skill overpowered 2 of the assailants whilst the other two escaped. The police arrived and the two men were

arrested and Squire Federer was taken to hospital and after receiving treatment to his injuries was able to return to his home. My editor decided to accept this word for word for publication on Thursday. The local East Anglia Times the Daily paper had a slightly different story it read as follows: Two local residents of Halstead came to the rescue of Squire Federer of Gestingthorpe when he was attacked by a gang of criminals. The two unnamed local residents fought off the attackers and the squire was taken to hospital for treatment to multiple injuries. It was right at the bottom under the headline Squire Federer beaten up by criminal Gang.

Derek had phoned Squire Federer and phoned me at the echo office to say we were invited to his house for 6'30 pm for dinner and to bring our girl friends. I phoned Yvonne and gave her the news. We don't need to eat as we are invited for dinner" I told her. At five minutes after five we boarded the bus home and as we got off the bus in Halstead Derek and Rosemary were waiting for us and we got into the squires chauffeur driven car and within 15 minutes we had arrived at his large house which stood off the road and up a long drive. The house was so big more like a castle and this was where we had been invited for dinner.

A maid greeted us at the door and took our jackets and hats and showed us into the lounge. The squire was sitting in a large armchair and stood up to greet us. We could see that there were a few marks on his face and it seemed that he had stitches on his left cheek, and both his hands were partly bandaged.

We had a lovely meal at the hospitality of the squire and his French wife Simone. As we put on our coats on to leave he handed both Derek and I a cheque for 100 pounds each.

At first we both refused but he insisted had it not been for our intervention he might well have died on the street. This money was four months' wages for me so was gratefully received. As we got back into the car for our return home Yvonne snuggled up to me whispering in my ear "Dexter my special hero" I think Rosemary was giving due to praise to Derek and this cash would certainly help out for their wedding in Manchester in October.

Derek came into my room after knocking on the door "Free to chat brother" he exclaimed as he entered. He sat on the bed next me and began "Rose told me that Von (as he called Yvonne) had talked to her about contraceptives" "Don't tell dad" I interrupted. Derek put his hand on my shoulder "You know me better than that I am not like Dean I know he tells Dad everything trivial or not" He paused, put his hand in his inside pocket and gave me a packet and explained "Use these, but only once, one for each time and dispose of it. So nobody can find it not down the toilet, but in the dustbin in a bag right down the bottom of the bin, so it cannot be found." He smiled "enjoy yourself, I do" and he winked as he left the room. Inside the box were 3 balloon like objects and instructions on how to use them printed on a slip of paper inside. I decided to hide this box in a secret place where mum or dad would not find it. My secret place was under the carpet by the window where a loose floorboard could be lifted up and beneath it I hid the box in a cake tin. It was where everything I wanted kept private would be located.

The court case against the 4 assailants on the Squire took place the following week and they were all sent down for 3 months having been charged with the attack and had previous form which they had been found guilty in Halstead and surrounding district. The police had found the other two culprits involved in the attack as The Squire had identified them at an earlier identification parade which both Derek and myself attended and recognised the men.

It was not until late October that Yvonne and I were able to make use of the gift given to me by Derek. I often spent time in my girlfriend's room without being disturbed by her parents as we listened to records and a little fumble and tumble on the bed whilst remaining fully dressed but hands inside each other's clothing. This was a means of satisfaction but not to the extent we really wanted. George told me they were going up to Manchester to meet some relations of Connie, and wanted me to stay in their house with their daughter again for the Saturday night.

We went to the station to see Yvonne's parents off to Manchester and walked arm in arm back to her home. We had both discussed what we would do and were both excited at this prospect of taking our love to the ultimate conclusion. We wasted no time going up to her bedroom and made certain that on advice from Rose to put under ourselves towels that could be washed so that any tell-tale signs of her virginity fluids and any fluid from me would be eradicated. We undressed each other slowly and gently kissing each part of the body as it was exposed. We did not use Derek's gift for a while, as we enjoyed the foreplay. At the right time she put the gift onto the part of the body it was intended for and we did that deed that we both desired and enjoyed. My love for Yvonne was growing stronger and stronger and she never missed an opportunity to tell me how much she loved me and I would say the same I love you or often in Tagalog *Mahal Kita lubos* (I love you completely). Having enjoyed our romantic liaison, we lay in bed naked together cuddling and kissing before we both fell asleep and only for the second time in almost 5 months we had slept and woken together in the same bed.

We awoke at 9 am and enjoyed sharing a shower together. It was the first time we had washed each other and we both enjoyed this experience as we could show that we had no inhibitions in any respect where our bodies were concerned. Having taken a breakfast of Bacon and Eggs, marmalade on toast and cups of tea whilst dressed only in our dressing gowns. We did eventually dress in our Sunday best to go to church for the 11am service.

Back from church the news on the TV was full of the uprising in Hungry. We watched as the revolt started with student demonstration which attracted thousands as it marched through Budapest to the parliament. A student delegation entered the radio station to broadcast their demands. When the demonstrators outside demanded the delegation's release, the police fired at them. Violence erupting throughout the capital, and throughout the country. Thousands were fighting the State Security Police Reports of Pro-Soviet communists were being executed by former prisoner who were released and armed. As they tried to take control of the government and local councils from the ruling workers party.

During the news we watched, Yvonne was laying on my lap rubbing her bottom against my crotch. It was evident that she was anxious to continue what we had done last night. It was just as well that there were another two rubbers left in the box. We were so anxious to continue our love making that we undressed ourselves quickly and got between the sheets. Foreplay first then the deed that I was able to make last before we dropped off to sleep that afternoon. We were only disturbed when the door was unlocked and we heard the voices of George and Connie. We dressed so quickly that we were downstairs before her parents had taken off their coats, and sitting on the sofa pretending to be asleep when they entered. Yvonne made pretend that she was going to the bathroom whilst in fact she went into her bedroom to remove the bed sheets and replace them but she told me later that they looked OK so did not have to change them. She slipped the used condom into my pocked and whispered in my ear "Get rid of it as soon as you can darling, you know what I mean".

It was just after 10 pm when I walked home from Yvonne's house and had forgotten to dispose of the used condom. It was not until I was getting ready for bed that I felt it inside my pocket. I pulled it out and accidentally snared it on my keys in my pockets spilling the content onto the floor. I quickly cleaned it up and remembered what Derek had told me about where I should put it after it was used. I waited until the rest of the household was asleep and stole out of the house to put it in the dustbin. Unfortunately, the front door closed behind me and there I was in my dressing and slippers outside in the coldness of the evening, I looked around for an open window and the only window open was that of my sister Denise. It would mean a climb up the drainpipe to reach her room. I checked that the pipe would take my weight and slowly climbed up and pulled my body through the window as quietly as I could so as not to disturb my sister. I was on the floor and it was dark as I moved slowly towards the bedroom door. I caught my foot on the side of a chair and it fell to the floor. I sighed with temporary relieve that my sister did not stir. I placed the chair upright and proceeded to the door just as the light came on. My sister exclaimed "Dexter what are you doing in my room?" I had to think quickly and stated "You know that Christian book you borrowed from me I wanted it back as there was something I needed to read in it and it was a worry to me I could not remember what it said about David and Goliath" Denise laughed. "I gave you the book back last week, so what is the real reason you climbed through my window." I sat on her bed and offered to tell her the truth if she promised not to tell Dad or mum. Or Yvonne's parents "OK tell me" she demanded "and I promise as God is my witness not to tell our parents, or Yvonne's parents. Well! I began "Derek gave me something to use when I was with Yvonne" She smiled enough said I can guess what it was he gave me some to use with my Gordon, but why you climbing through my window". When I gave her the full story of my concern about the condom, she stifled a laugh for fear of waking our parents. I went back to my bedroom and slept almost immediately dreaming that Yvonne was beside me.

I met Yvonne at the bus stop and a few people that passed us bye told us that the buses were on strike told us. We had to go by train from Halstead to Chappel and Wakes Colne then change onto the Gainsborough line to Colchester. The slowness of the train and several prolonged stops at Earls Colne and White Colne before arriving at Chappel and Wakes Colne and waiting for the Colchester train coming in from Sudbudy. We were both late for work. The trains quite understandably because of the bus strike were packed to the rafters and we had to stand all the way to Colchester. We had to come back the same way that night and two further days, as the strike did not finish until Thursday. It was a dispute over the sacking of a driver for a passenger claimed he was drunk whilst driving the bus from Sible Hedingham to Halstead. Nothing was proved and the bus company reinstated the driver through lack of evidence. Later it turned out that it was a woman who had an affair with the driver then found out he was married so she and another person made up the fictional story he was drunk as retribution for his infidelity.

I'd been playing football for Halstead reserves for 2 seasons and the first Saturday in November I was called up to play in the first team at Colchester Layer road. In the third round of the FA cup Halstead had won the first round against Haverhill and the second round against Edgware Town; It was a great honour at my age of 16 and 11 months to play in our first team. Remember (subs were not allowed in 1956) they were not permitted until the 65 66 season.

Yvonne always liked to watch me play in the home games and sometimes away. This was a big match for me and she wanted to be there. I would only be the second Barren to paly for the first team as Derek before he went to university played regularly in the first team as centre half. My position was left half or right half depending on what position the Manager wanted me to play. I was excited but I did not know what position I would occupy since the two regular half backs were out injured.

This was the first time I had walked onto the Layer road pitch at Colchester, although I had been to see a few matches there if they were on a Friday night. Normally I was playing for Halstead Reserves or youth team on Saturdays. So unless I was injured myself I would not be able to see them on Saturday. (No Sunday football in those days) The Manager put his arm round me in the dressing room "Barren my son you are playing on the left wing go out and give me 100 percent I know you can do it I know you don't play wing front often but I think you got the speed and stamina to take it in your stride.

It was the biggest crowd I had ever played in front of almost 12,000 standing we were lucky to get 100 or less to watch a reserve match, although the first team would have a 1000 or more at most matches and cup games at home would be a capacity 3000.

We were pegged back in our own half for much of the opening 20 minutes and Colchester had 5 good shots on goal but our keeper Lee Parker was in fine form. We had good possession in the last 10 minutes and our Centre forward Dick Ridgewell almost scored but his shot was cleared off the line by their right back. We concluded the first half honours even at no goals each. The second half in the first 5 minutes was blistering for us as I was gifted a cross from our Centre half Doug Yeldham and took it on my right food and from 12 yard out slammed the ball into the back of the net. It was the only break we got as for the remainder of the half we were under siege as shot after shot sailed towards our goal most off target but the few that got towards the goal. Lee Parker was in fine form and come the final whistle a last gasp two fisted save by Lee gave us the match 1.0. Lee piped me as man of the match but I got praise enough from my team mates, despite the fact that I had not really played my best. I was included in the next two matches but failed to impress at this higher level and dropped and not recalled until the last senior match of the season. An insignificant match win or lose would not alter our position in the league as we had already won the championship. Most of the reserve players were included and we were not expected to win but we did 4 0 and I scored twice from the left wing position. The first I scored after their right back slipped and the keep came off his line to quickly and I hoisted the ball over his head. The second was from the penalty spot when Mark Digwell was upended in the box. The captain Neil Fletcher asked me to take the spot kick much to my surprise. I had taken penalties before for the reserves and never missed. I thought I had kicked it too slow and the keeper was right behind it but it bounced out of his hands and crossed the line into the goalmouth. That was goal number 4 for Halstead Town.

Chapter 5

THE FAMILY WEDDING OF THE YEAR

It was Derek and Rosemary's big day. The family wedding of the year and of course I was not playing football that weekend. We travelled up to Manchester by train., with several changes and having left at 4 30 pm on Friday night we never arrived in Manchester until 10 30 pm. Today the same trip but going from Braintree station to Manchester would take 4 hours or less (The Halstead station and Colne Valley line closed on the 30th of December 1961.)

We were booked into the Britannia hotel one of the oldest hotels in Manchester and not far from the railway station. Yvonne and I were given adjacent rooms. What my parents did not know, there was an adjoining door between the two rooms, I thought it was locked but to my delight it opened and I had one condom left. We were booked in at this hotel for 2 nights all at Dad's expense including Denise's boyfriend Gordon and my Yvonne. Derek was staying in the hotel as well, his future wife at home with her parents. Only Dean on his own but Derek kept him company. I had to thank my big brother again as he slipped me another packet of 3 and I assumed he gave the same to Denise to give to Gordon. As he had reiterated some time ago. "It is safer to use condoms than to get the woman pregnant". He was looking after his families' moral position, knowing that if either Denise or Yvonne were to be pregnant out of wedlock the disgrace it would bring on the family . The head of the family our father was a well-respected Reverend and short-listed to be a Bishop.

As it was late we all retired to our rooms, without further delay. I opened the adjoining door to Yvonne's room and she was already waiting for me dressed in a full length night dress and as I flung the door open she fell into my arms and lifting her gently in my arms I carried her onto her bed.
"Is it safe my darling?" She whispered pausing for my reply "Yes it is my parents are on the next floor on the far side of the hotel" I told her. She then she pulled the night dress over her head to display her radiant charms that I had come to love so much. I took off my pyjamas and together we lay on the bed. I learned over to where my pyjamas were on the chair and too out the condom from the top pocket. "Not yet darling let's just kiss and cuddle". She requsted. So that's what we did until later as the city clock struck 1 am she helped me fit the condom., and the duty of love making to the fullest extent was consumed. We slept in the sheets together knowing that if my parents were to come up and see us they would have to knock first and this would

give us time for me to return to my bed. I had already before coming into Yvonne's bed laid in my bed to give the impression I had slept in it (Sorry forget to mention both the bedrooms had double beds). A knock on the door brought us both awake and a voice called out. It is 8 am Madam, if you want breakfast it will finish in half an hour." "Thank you sir" Yvonne replied. I rushed into my room just as the same voice called out "Breakfast finishes in half an hour sir" Thanks I will be down in time "I replied and added for good measure "did you knock next door to my girlfriend?" "Yes indeed young sir and she replied." He informed me, I did this just in case there might be some suspicion on behalf of the unseen voice that we shared the same room which was strictly against the Hotel police. We dressed in our wedding suits and went down for breakfast. Fruit juice to start then cornflakes, egg and bacon with a friend slice. This followed by toast and marmalade not to forget a pot of tea complete with strainer (tea bags not available in 1956).

My father was invited to marry Derek and Rosemary at 12 pm at St Luke's Church. *(A Grade 2* listed, building among the top 10% of buildings in England. Prominent because of its position and its slender, continental-style spire, it stands on a small green hill beside Liverpool Street – and is known locally as "the church on the hill". People worship there on Sunday mornings, and most newcomers find them friendly and welcoming. Inside the church's most spectacular feature is the decorated roof over the chancel, and it is blessed with a fine organ. Just down the hill was the Parish Hall,)*

Over 100 guests attended this wedding. The Reception was held down the hill at the parish hall. Derek and Rosemary now a married couple left the reception just after 3 pm en route for their honeymoon on the island of Cyprus. It was after 6 pm when we as a family minus Derek and Rosemary returned to the Britannia Hotel. We all skipped dinner as we had enough to eat at the reception. We sat down as a family and our Father led us in prayer for the married couple.

It was not too late when we retired to bed again and after kissing our parents good night I casually asked my father

"When can Yvonne and I get engaged" He chuckled to himself "funny you should ask that Dexter, Gordon asked me for the hand of your sister in marriage" and! I intersected. "What was your answer" "If Gordon asks her and she accepts I can see no reason to say no, and if you ask Yvonne's parents and they say yes then you and her have my blessing as well. He took hold of my arm "If you get married make it next year and you might like to consult with Denise for perhaps a joint engagement and wedding. He suggested with a snug smile.

I opened the packet of condoms and lay one on the table beside the bed. I opened the door to Yvonne's room (yes gratefully it was still unlocked) "My bed tonight darling" I exclaimed as I stood in the doorway in just my y fronts. Yvonne was already in just her underwear and taking off her bra covered her breasts with both her hands before pushing both upwards. I walked towards her and hugged her as tight as I could. "You know I asked my Dad if and when we can get engaged he gave his blessing, but first I must ask your father for your hand" A broad smile crept over her face "I asked my parents if we could get engaged and his words were as soon as Dexter asks you to marry him I will give him your hand" she paused "but you get more than my hand you get my body and soul and my love for a lifetime. I went down on one knee and she laughed "you don't have to do that the answer is yes" She repeated it thrice more each time louder than the last so that probably everyone in the hotel heard her. I scooped her into my arms and carried her into my room and onto my bed both of us removing from each our last item of clothing before slipping between the sheets.

Our foreplay was intense even better than 3 previous times. We experimented letting our mouths explore the parts never seen in public, before pulling on the condom and completing our love marking and then side by side cuddled up close together. Prolonging a kiss in which we tasted each other's mouths with tongue-to-tongue wrestling. We were so happy and a life of pleasure lay ahead of us.

We returned home and we told George and Connie about

our visit to Manchester. We omitted our sexual encounters. I sat down and spoke to George directly "I want to marry Yvonne, so may I ask for her hand in marriage" George looked at me with no expression on his face and turned to face Connie. Connie without any facial expression looked at me then to Yvonne and back to George and I felt nervous in anticipation of his reply. "What do you think Con should we let this young man have our daughters hand or shall I tell him he is not good enough for our little girl." My heart sunk, as I observed no reaction on either of Yvonne's parents' faces. It seemed like forever that I waited for an answer. At last George broke the silence and took his wife's hand in his kissed her on the lips and looked at Yvonne and myself as we were not seated on the sofa together holding hands. "Of course Dexter you can marry Yvonne, but please wait until you June next year when you have been together a year," I stood up and shook hands with both George and Connie and she kissed me and Yvonne as did George and I sealed this good news with a kiss to the lips of my intended.

It came about during a family discussion that Denise and Gordon went along with my father's suggestion that we have a joint wedding in June with an engagement party after my birthday in December. In actual fact the date chosen was my birthday and all the family were there to celebrate.

My second best present was my grandfather's gift of a course of driving lessons. The first gift was Yvonne as to be my wife in 1957. From the day on I was to call her Von and her pet name for me was Dex.

Our Christmas together was quite frantic and combine with a joint engagement of my sister Denise her fiancé Gordon and Yvonne and myself. This would be Derek's last Christmas before he enlisted into the army for his national service. He would undertake this training as an officer at Sandhurst in Surrey. In January, because of his medical internship his enlistment had been deferred until he was qualified as a doctor. His wife Rosemary was already pregnant and the expected birth of their first child was in August 1957.

In January Von celebrated her 17th birthday and in February 1957 I passed my driving test at the first time of asking. I managed to purchase and Austin A30 in black a four-door saloon built in 1951. It only cost me 80 pounds from a lady who had been advised by her doctor to give up driving as she was suffering from advance stages of inoperable glaucoma. With the tax and insurance, I was left with just five pounds of the hundred given to me by the squire, plus the interest of course. The day I brought the car I took Von for a spin to see my grandfather's and to thank him for his gift of driving lessons that enabled me to pass my test and buy my first car.

After we left my Grandparent's home we decided to park in a meadow. The reason for this was obvious we wanted to christen the car. We open the rear doors and positioned ourselves on the back seat. I removed my trousers and pants and Von slipped out of her knickers. I unwrapped the last condom and with Von's help it was fixed onto my appendage. I was well away and close to climax when I looked out of the back window. A tractor was only a few yards away it was bearing down towards us. No time to complete my seduction as I leapt out of the car to the front seat and switched on the engine. It stalled and now this tractor oblivious of us in its line of travel was less than 10 years from us I pulled Von out of the car as she had already out on her knickers. Handbrake off we managed to push the car out of harm's way as the Tractor ploughed through the bushes across the road and entered she ditch on the other side of the road. Its rear wheels in the air. I hastily raced across the road and jumped on the tractor and switched the engine off before attending to the driver who was in a semi consciousness state. I was certain that he had either had a heart attack or a stroke. I called "Von go down the road and in 100 yards there is a red phone box dial 999 and tell the operator you need an ambulance on the Sampford Road 1 mile from Hempstead village."

Ten minutes later the ambulance arrived and followed by a police car. With the assistance of the two police officers they lifted the man out of the tractor and into the ambulance. One of the police officers confirmed that the driver experienced a stroke. We have the police a statement and they went over to my car. He looked inside the car and looked back at me

I assumed that he noticed the condom packet on the seat,"

I dare say you were having a romantic liaison in your car." The senior older officer chuckled. "why do you think" that I asked nervously. He put his arm round me and laughed "Don't worry son you are not going to get into trouble, in fact praise as you might just have saved the drivers life" He paused and continued" I was young once and I understand you love your young lady, and at least you parked off the road and not in the public eye" We are getting married in June" I retorted. Both police officers laughed and the younger one said "Then when you are man and wife you won't need to do it in car" He leaned inside the car and picked up the condom packet and suggested "Don't let her parents see this, and by the way where is the rubber. I touched my flies realizing in my panic to move the car it was still attached. The officers both smiled and returned to their car. My little A30 started OK and we went home.

I earned the nickname NEWSHAWK from my editor as for the fourth time I had been involved a newsworthy incident. The headline of this incident in the Echo slightly adjusted read TRACTOR DRIVER SUFFERS STROKE. Our cub reported Dexter Barren was once making the news he was driving his car along the road towards Hempstead when he saw a tractor drive into a ditch. Dexter's quick of thought in jumping up into the tractor to switch off the engine saved the tractor driver who had a stroke whilst driving through a meadow and across a main road and planted his vehicle face down into a ditch. Dexter's girlfriend called the ambulance and the driver Mark Williams who worked for local farmer Reg Winters was taken to the hospital where he is said to be comfortable and out of danger. This incident happens on the Great Sampford Road in Hempstead last Saturday afternoon. A few days later I received a letter from both Mr Winters and Mark's wife thanking me for my actions.

Chapter 6

HONEYMOON IN BOURNEMOUTH

Two weeks before our wedding and Von passed her driving test and I let her drive the car. "Where shall we go?" she asked as she switched on the engine and looked into my eyes, "Where you want" I suggested. Von drove the car to the former Ridgewell aerodrome where on a few occasions I had taken her for some extra driving lessons. It was there I recollected we had entered one of the nissan huts with a blanker and there on the floor did make love using the condom I failed to fill on our last try in the car in Hempstead. I checked before using it that it had not suffered any ruptures or tears. The last thing I wanted on that day in March was the thing to burst. If it had and Von was pregnant she would have gone up the aisle over 3 months pregnant. It was quite warm on that day in march and we gave ourselves to each other totally naked under the blanket and on an old mattress we found in the hut. She the more anxious than I as she sat on my lap as I lay horizontal on the mattress. As she reached her climax she screamed out "Dexter Barren I love you I love you so much I want you in my life and in my body. I groaned too with pleasure too as together it was a mutual climax. I did the decent thing after we finished and disposed of the used condom by burning it.

Unlike the other lovers who just left their condoms strewn in the corner of the hut.

We stopped on the aerodrome where the lover's nissan hut had been. Obviously it along with the other huts had been demolished. However, the tower was still there but was locked up securely. We were anxious to make love so with no building available we satisfied our carnal desires in the back seat of the car just removing our lower garments it was to be the last time that I was to use a condom, for in two weeks' time we would be married.

As my father was conducting the service in St. Andrews church for our joint wedding it was my grandfather who gave Denise away to Gordon. George did the same honours for Von. My brother Dean was best man and his new girlfriend Sally Turner was one of the four bridesmaids. Derek attended the wedding in his army uniform with wife Rosemary seven months pregnant. The reception was held in the White Hart hotel and went on until early evening. Denise and Gordon left for their honeymoon to Blackpool 20 minutes before us and were going by train. Von and myself followed and they decorated our car with ribbons on tin cans and the traditional board that read **JUST MARRIED**.

Petron rationing, which has been in force in Britain for five months following the Suez crisis, has finally been abolished. There were loud cheers in the House of Commons when the Paymaster General Reginald Maudling made the announcement that restrictions had been lifted because stocks were "at a satisfactory level".

We were spending our nuptials in Bournemouth thankfully petrol rationing had ended in the May of 57 otherwise we could not have purchased sufficient petrol for this trip. It was late when we arrived at The Imperial Hotel in Bournemouth and after booking in we went straight to bed. This was the first time we would make love without the need of a condom. I got into bed first totally naked and excited at the prospect of making love properly, flesh to flesh without a rubber to catch the sperm. Von came out of the bathroom wearing a white nylon long nightdress. "You not wearing that are you" I enquired. She smiled at me as she stepped out of it to reveal her hourglass figure mesmerized me wearing only her engagement and wedding rings. In the half-light she gently turned round slowly lifting her arms above her head to tease me and to make me more excited. I was so aroused I could not wait for her to enter the big king size bed. I pushed back the sheet and stepped out of the bed and embraced her with my arms round her back and my sex pressed against her body lifted her onto the bed. We kissed passionately before she took my sex to the entrance of her secret place. With her below me I entered for the first time with naked flesh. I could feel myself inside here and with our joint climax it was a night to remember. Oh yes!

The morning so more sexual activity but during the night we slept in each other's arms. Many times during that night our lips were locked together even to taking each other's tongue into our own mouths. Hands often wandering to the unseen parts to stimulate. We skipped breakfast. It was past midday when we emerged from our love nest and a brisk walk along the front where we purchased 20 Rothman's cigarettes. For the first time in my life the Polish guy who owned the tobacconists introduced me to smoking a pipe. He took out a wooden briar pipe and asked "Young sir have you ever thought about smoking one of these" I nodded my head I smoke the occasional cigar but never tried a pipe" He was a good salesman as convinced me that a pipe was a status symbol. I paid for the pipe and an ounce of Condor tobacco. *(To this day I still smoke a pipe and the odd cigar but never a cigarette any more)*

We spent the rest of the afternoon on the beach and did not realize that we had not eaten any food since we left the reception. We were both ravenous at dinner, and even asked for extra vegetables to even having a second sweet. The head waiter realized we had both missed breakfast and lunch. We had paid for full board so he could not complain at our request for extra portions. We stayed in the lounge to watch television for a while before we retired to bed at 9 pm. Von reminded me that in all the excitement of wedding and our indulgent romance, not only had we missed going to church but failed to phone our parents. We made love that night as if our very lives depended upon it.

In the morning we took as shower together. I spread the soap down both Von's legs slowly with both hands and washed both feet as she lifted up each one in turn. My fingers eased between her toes that made her squirm a little, as it seemed I was tickling her. As I turned her body round to face me I covered her petite breasts with my soapy hands. Downwards to the tummy gently fingering her navel before sliding my right hand down to her pubic hair and onto her body inlets rear and front. A finger in each. I could see the smile on her face and her obvious enjoyment as I pushed my lips on to her open mouth.

Now it was my new wife's turn to was my body. Taking the soap and in complete silence of words only groans of pleasure from me she rubber her soap hand onto my firm and solid manhood. She knelt down in front of me and engulfed my love stick into her mouth, Whilst her hands now soaped my chest. My own sexual fluids mixed with the soap and cascading water as she removed my appendage from her mouth shortly after it had erupted. Stepping out of the shower we dried each other's body before went down to the restaurant for a well-deserved breakfast after our exhilarating erotic, yet romantic activity.

We spent Monday on beach all day. The same for Tuesday and in both nights we enjoyed each other's body. Like an express train. Hardly a minute would pass by when we did not kiss. We spent some time window-shopping. We even drove the car to Swanage saw Corfe Castle and wandered. Around Poole and saw the largest natural in the UK. Wednesday it was a little cloudy so we went to the cinema in the afternoon to see Elves Presley film Love me tender. We sat in the back seat and enjoyed several kissing sessions.

Wednesday morning the Hotel manager called us to one side "Mr. Barren can I have a word with you and your lady?" He requested. "Yes you can but the lady is my wife she is Mrs. Barren since Saturday 3pm" I replied sarcastically. The manager coughed "No insult intended I do assure you both" he paused "I have to ask you to leave the hotel today as soon as possible" "Why? what have we done we are booked here until Friday night. You wrote to us and confirmed the booking in May" I interrupted. "Are we making too much noise or what?" I continued. The manager shook his head "No nothing like that, you have been model guests, but we overlooked that you are double booked with" he paused and continued "A VIP who regularly stays here and always has the honeymoon suite, and their business I cannot afford to lose" "So what alternatives have you got, another room here or another hotel?" I enquired indignantly. The managed rubbed his chin and explained. "It is not simple as that we don't not have any more rooms to let, and all the other hotels I contacted are fully booked, but I have arranged for you to say at a Guest house on Holdenhurst Road.. No charge to you of course, and we will pay for your stay in this Guest House and reimburse you for the days you will not stay here. That's 3 nights at three pound is that OK?" he asked. I shook my head "it's not good enough I will pay you £5.00 that's all and you still pay for the 3 nights in the other place if it meets with our approval" I insisted. The managed pushed the hair of his eyes and exclaimed "I can't do that" "Then Mr. Manager" I retorted. "We will not leave here until Saturday morning you have to honour our contract with us or you will face the consequences". I retorted with anger in my voice. "I am a journalist you know, and the adverse publicity would not do your hotel any good at all". I showed him my press card. His face turned bright red. He put his hands up "Stay here please." I will see what I can do for you I will go and see the owner. He departed quickly along the passage and we waited. Von smiled at me "No flies on you my darling husband".

The manager returned less than five minutes later. "Mr. and Mrs. Barren I am pleased to inform you the owner Mrs. Parker Davis has said I can fully reimburse you, for the 4 nights you spent here £12.00 is that right?" He paused "But you would pay half towards the room in Holdenhurst Road. He suggested, I thought for a few seconds and asked Von "Do you think that is fair darling?" "It's up to you" she replied. I extended my hand towards the manager and he shook it. "I take it we have a deal." He enquired with sense of relief on his face.

We drove the car to the address in Holdenhurst Road almost opposite the Dolphin public house and I knocked on the door. From the exterior the place looked unkempt, but I was reserving judgement until we saw the inside. A woman in her last 40's dressed in a scruffy torn blue dress open the door a cigarette dangling from her mouth. She spoke with the cigarette still dangling from the corner of her mouth.

"You the couple from the Imperial?" "Yes" I replied. She stood to one side and beckoned us to enter. "This way me dears" she sniffled as she led us up the creaky stairs with a well-worn carpet, evidence of its age in the amount of scuffs marks in the centre of the steps. We climbed 3 sets of stairs before opposite the last flight she opened the door to a dimly lit room. Wallpaper was peeling off the wall next to the single window that looked out onto a garden obscured by a tree with its branches almost touching the cracked windowpane and a large damp patch on the ceiling. Von tugged my shoulder and nodded her head downwards. We were standing on a damp patch. I did not need to ask if she wanted to stay here. "No, it's not for us thank you" I exclaimed. "Why? What's wrong with it, you won't get anywhere else in the town this time of year" I was angry at being offered such a disgusting room "I would not let my grandfather's pigs stay here yet alone us" I retorted. I could see she was angry and as she huffed and puffed and uttered many obscenities, we fled down the stairs and back to our car. We found a phone box just outside the Dolphin public house where I phoned box the manager of the Imperial and told him our thoughts on this guest house. I was surprised when he interrupted me to say. "That is my dear Mother's house" I put the phone down instantly. We did not bother to find another place to stay but decided to return home.

Chapter 7

HER BODY LANGUAGE CONFIRMED THE GOOD NEWS

Rather than go back to Halstead, we decided to go to my Grandfather's farm in Hempstead. *Hempstead is the birthplace of the notorious highwayman Richard (Dick) Turpin 1705 to 1739 executed in York. It is also the burial ground of Doctor William Harvey who discovered how blood circulates around the body. 1570 to 1657.* My grandparents were surprise to see me. Von was still in the car looking for the gifts we had purchased for family members. "Where in your wife you had a row and left her in Bournemouth on her own already". My grandmother exclaimed. I shook my head and pointed to the car as Von was walking towards the gate with their presents in her hand.

I then spent the next 15 to 20 minutes explaining what we did on our honeymoon (obviously not our sexual activity) and the problems at the hotel and the disgusting guesthouse. Both my grandparents laughed. "You are a shrewd operator young Dexter" suggested my grandfather. Grandmother was cooking for us, as we had not eaten since leaving Bournemouth. Fresh eggs that were laid that day, chips made from potatoes from her garden and cold ham off the bone from one of Grandfather's own pigs. And fresh cooked bread made by my Grandmother's fair hands. Von admitted it was just as good as her Father baked at his bakery in Castle Hedingham. We were just about to tuck into this delicious meal when the phone rang. My grandfather answered it and his end of the conversation went like this: yes this is Mr. Sam Portslade how can I help you? ...... Yes, I have read the letter .... No, what you have offered is not enough, anyway I do not want to sell you the two acres at the roadside end as how would I get my cows to milk through the residents back gardens... So you would give me access to herd the cows to the milking shed. Between the new houses you build at the near side. Of the field .... I don't think they would take kindly to my bovines shuffling through past their houses at 6 am every morning and at 3 in the afternoon .... Tell you what you make me a better offer and you take all 5 acres and I can move my cows to another field. .... OK you do that". Grandfather then told me that Humphrey and Williams a development company want to build a number of house on his five-acre site of which they had already obtained planning permission. The money offered was not sufficient and he would rather let the whole field go and buy the 3 acre field offered to him by Farmer Alfred Green at a very reasonable price which he could then move the milking sheds closer. Alfred Green had recently lost his wife and neither of his sons or grandkids wanted to inherit the farm when he died so slowly but surely he wanted to sell parts of it off. Grandfather had already purchased some farm equipment, a crop field along with some of his livestock, which he had integrated with his present stock.

We had just finished the meal when the phone rang again it was my brother Dean phoning from the school of agriculture where he had just been enrolled. He just wanted to tell our grandfather how much he was enjoying it and had made some good friends. No sooner had he returned the receiver to the cradle than he had to pick it up again. It was the construction company they agreed to buy all 5 acres and improved offer at eight thousand pounds. My father Grandfather smiled "Well eight grand will do me I can buy Green's field for two thousand that's what he wanted and give you my grandkids a grand each. And your mother another grand". But why is Green letting his 4-acre field going so cheap?" I asked "it's in the middle of four ten-acre crop fields one of them mine, so the value is low as there is no road access." So how will that benefit you?" I asked quizzically. Grandfather raised his finger "simple my boy, I keep Green's 4-acre field as a crop field as it is now and cordon off part of my crop field on the Great Sampford road as a meadow for the cows". He concluded.

As we drove to Halstead, Von touched my arm and kissed me on the cheek. "I know where you get your shrewdness from, your grandfather", I laughed "I guess so." No flies on me or my grandfather.

As we reached the village of Finchingfield, I let Von drive the rest of the way home. Like my grandparents George and Connie were surprise to see us at this time. I let Von tell the story of our visit and complications in Bournemouth. As George had paid for our honeymoon hotel and in the end it cost us nothing, I offered him the twenty-one pounds that was reimbursed to us. He declined suggesting we put it towards the petrol down to Bournemouth and back.

We went to my parent's home where the same story was repeated. Dad had a phone call from Derek to inform him that he had been called up for his national service. His conscription had been deferred until he had complete his internship as a doctor. He would of course undertake his two years compulsory conscription as a medical officer, spending six weeks at Sandhust. *The royal military academy is located on the boarder of Surrey and Berkshire opened in*

1947. At least Derek would not be posted out to Korea as the war was almost over and by the time he finished his training, our boys would be coming home. I realized that I would not be deferred and come January I would without doubt be starting my national service. I had already made up my mind I would, if given a choice go into the RAF.

Von thought she might pregnant come July. I was not surprised since she had the traditional morning sickness and I encourage her to see the Doctor. I waited outside the clinic whilst I listened to the radio in our car. It was too hot for me inside the surgery, anyway with so many patients in there I would have to stand up, so opted for being in the car with the windows open. Von was covering her face when she came out of the surgery. Was she or was she not with her face covered there was no way of telling. Not until she reached the car did she remove her hand and I saw a big grin on her face I was out of the car and she threw her arms round me kissing me full on the lips. No need for me to ask, her body language confirmed the good news. Her parents were the first to hear the news followed by my parents grandparents Denise and Gordon, Derek and Rosemary and last of all Dean who told his girlfriend Sally. The baby would be born in late February. It seemed our first bundle of joy was conceived whilst we were on honeymoon. Three days later, Denise announced she too was pregnant. And on the 31st of January, Rosemary gave birth to a bouncing baby boy she and Derek name him Arthur John Wilson. He was my first nephew and was excited at being an Uncle. On the 6th of February, our son Aqyza Barren was born.
Not much really happened during the summer that was out of the ordinary. Our frequent visits to the river to sunbathe and swim. A few seaside trips to Walton on the Naze, Clacton, Frinton, Felixstowe and Maldon. We also made a few excursions into London and to see Derek at his passing our parade at Sandhurst, we made two visits to Dean at the Agriculture College in Grantham Lincolnshire. All this would not have been possible until petrol rationing ended in May 1957.

Dean and myself helped grandfather with the harvest and

it was then when he gave Dean and myself the thousand pounds each for the sale of his five-acre field just past the Rose and Crown and Wilshires the family store. I would often go to the pub or store for my grandfather to get him a bottle of wine or 20 woodbines or weights cigarettes. He suffered weights but his favourite was woodbines.

Christmas 1957 was held at my parent's house all the family attended. Derek in his officer's uniform looked magnificent, but I felt sorry for Gordon who had also started his conscription, and was only in his other ranks uniform as a gunner in the royal artillery. Other ranks do not socialise with officers. This was a family occasion and knowing the uneasy feeling of Gordon Derek went upstairs and changed into his civilian clothes. Denise went back to her cottage close by and fetched Gordon's wedding suit so he would not look out of place and more at ease. Boxing day and I spent it with Von's parents. This was also my home. The thousand pound given to by my grandfather was put into a high interest savings account, so that after I finished my conscription would go towards our own home.

As expected, I started my conscription and went to the Royal Air force college Cranwell in Lincolnshire for a six-week officer-training course. *In the latter half of the 20th century, it was gradually increased to 32 weeks. Compulsory conscription was ended in 1960.* I made many friends there and many of them are still friends today. I was after training commission as a flying officer and 6 months later promoted to Flight lieutenant. From my training at Cranwell, I was to be based at RAF Stanmore. My linguistic talents were to be of great use to be service. To encourage me to extend to a three-year term they offered me a big increase in my salary. I accepted and by the end of the second year further promotion to squadron leader. I was then posted to RAF Bruggen in Germany for 6 months a communications officer.

"I was more than upset when I found out that this Welshman was touching my girlfriend up. I did not intend to do what I did; it was in a fit of rage. I picked up this empty beer bottle and smashed it against the wall then I crushed it into his face, as you know. I had never seen so much blood pouring out of a man's face or the skin tear so easily. As I pulled the bottle back I was shocked to see that one of his eyeballs was attached to the bottle. I dropped the bottle and ran" This was the statement of the young airman I was asked to defend at a court martial. He had been asked which officer should represent him and he had asked for Squadron Leader Barren.

I had visited the welsh airman in hospital. He was undergoing surgery later that day to try and save his eyesight but the scares on his face would be permanent. I was going to defend his assailant but in all honesty having seen the Welsh airman's face I did not feel I could defend such an animal for the damage he had done to a fellow human being. All I could do was plead that he had remorse for his actions. The day of the trial and he was convicted of the heinous crime and sent to Prison for 10 years and a discharge from the RAF.

I had played in all four soccer matches for RAF Bruggen, and my skill had not gone unnoticed by the RAF Germany manager. I was selected to play for the RAF team against The British Army team based in Germany. My normal position was a left-winger. In those far off days of the 60's the formation was of 1 2 3 5. The manager wanted me in the team but not as left wing but as inside left. Three other players from Bruggen would be in the team our Goal keeper Rick the right back Bob, Long John as centre back, and of course myself.

I will not spend too much time on my air force years in this book, maybe in a later novel. I don't want this book to have a comparison with Biggles the children's author Capt. W.E Johns whose books fascinated me in my youth. I did read most of Biggles books but not all I think he wrote over 100.

I was 21 by the time I had completed my service to my country, our bundle of joy Aqyza was a few months off his third birthday and Linda our little girl was also a few months away from her second year of age. During my stay at Stanmore Von and my kids joined me and we had a house in nearby Elstree provided by the RAF. We liked the area very much and we did consider moving to this part of Hertfordshire. When we could get baby sitters we often went out for a drink in our local pub the Wagon and Horses. A few of my air force buddies used to get there and we would play darts and snooker. I also played soccer for RAF Stanmore and attracted the interest of scouts from Arsenal and Watford football clubs. I was also a regular contributor to a number of local newspapers.

The RAF tried to persuade me to sign on for a further period of years I was one the youngest squadron leaders at 20 as most squadron leaders were 25 or older before reaching this rank.

At 21, I decided my whole life was ahead of me I had two choices in my professional life carry on as a journalist or become a pro soccer player. I had a trial for Arsenal at Highbury and though I gave a good account of myself scoring twice for the gunners in a reserve match against Watford they did not consider I was good enough to were the red and white of Arsenal. I was disappointed. A scout like to meet Matt Busby with a view to having a trial with his famous club. *(At this time he was one of the most successful managers in football and one of the longest serving having been their manager since 1945 that was 15 years in 1961 and his players generally known as the **Busby babes**. After his 1968 European cup final win, he retired.)* The idea of becoming a Busby babe did not really appeal to me, my club was Arsenal and if they did not think I was good enough, my choice would be to obtain work as a journalist.

I stayed at Von's parents home as I went back to work for the Echo. My career challenges led elsewhere as I wrote to a number of National papers I had written to the News Chronicle in 1960 but the day after I wrote the letter they merged with the Daily Mail. I got a nice letter back from the Editor-in-Chief of the Mail asking me to contact them again after I left the service. I did and went for an interview. I did not like their set up and the fact I would virtually be a tea boy or a go for meaning for whatever they wanted. I also had an interview with the News of the world and it was more or less same scenario. I got a letter completely out of the blue from the Peter Davis news agency in Perth Western Australia. They wanted to offer me a job as their correspondent in London.

Chapter 8

INTERNATIONAL CORRESPONDENT

I attended the interview in London at Australian house with Von. Peter Davis himself had flown over from down under to interview me personally. I was shown into his office and he asked us what we would like to drink, I requested coffee and Von asked for tea. Both milk and no sugar. He called out to a female assistant and told her to get one coffee and one tea. He never asked to see my references or credentials. "May I ask Sir how did you know about me? I never sent you my CV." Peter leaned back in his chair, his hands behind his neck smiled at us and remarked." I make it my business to find my own journalists and you have something special that will suit me perfectly and I want you on board." He paused "you were recommended to me by your editor at the Echo and a number of local newspapers you wrote for in London." He paused to clear his throat and continued. I have read a few of your reports before you went into the RAF in the Echo and a few from other news mediums you have had input, and I like what I read. You speak several languages which is a boost and if you write them as well it's a bonzer as we deal with a number of foreign language newspapers and that to me is very useful" He paused again and looked directly at me and asked "you do write the languages too, I take it". "All accept Chinese I write. He looked down at a paper on his desk and read "Spanish, French, Italian, German, Portuguese, Tagalog and English you write but not Mandarin" I interrupted "I suppose I could learn to write. No need so long as you can speak it clearly. We can always send a your voice transmission to the Chinese media" He suggested. Ten minutes later Von and myself left the interview and she held onto my arm tightly and kissed my cheek "So this is the job you really wanted" she asked. I kissed her full on the lips and commented. Yes! It is and with the salary he offered me and help with a house in London or near to London. I want it that's why I accepted." I could sense that Von was a little anxious but security for our young family and her was the important issue.

We found a house to rent in Stanmore and began negotiations to buy a three-bedroom house on a new estate in Borehamwood next to Elstree. We moved back to Stanmore not far from RAF Stanmore so was able to renew friendships with a lot of the guys still based there. It was my job to follow up on any major story in London also to form a friendship with the editor of Hansard the parliamentary newspaper. I was surprised to find that the assistant editor was an old air force chum from Sandhurst and we reacquainted ourselves over a few beers in the local tavern before a stroll along the north bank of the Thames.

Aqyza and Linda were growing up so fast and their curiosity was one of amazement. It was Aqyza's 3rd birthday on the 6th of February and ironically it was Linda's 2nd birthday just a year apart. Von was on the pill after the birth of Linda. We decided together that two kids would be enough. Both Rosemary and Denise settled for two. Dean had been considered for officer material and joined the Royal Navy.

He had spent a lot of his time abroad on three different ships. He was away on his last trip for 6 months but Sally never let her love for him vanish. They exchanged many letters over the course of two years as he wrote every day, but had to wait until his boat was in port before he could post them. Sally wrote every day, so strong was their love for each other. Dean had planned his wedding for after he came out of the navy after his two-year conscription. He finished in January 1961 exiting from the navy as a lieutenant. Five days after I was demobbed from the RAF. His agriculture training was put to good use in the navy as he oversaw all farming on board the ships he served. Some of the best-kept gardens on board ships won him special praise from two of the top Admirals. He married Sally in Halstead on Saturday the 4th of February. The entire family were there. He was guaranteed employment when he came back into civilian life as Grandfather's farm Manager. *(Later after Grandfather died he inherited the farm and agreed that he would over a few years pay the remainder of the family their equal share of the inheritance. We decline this genuine offer as we had our own careers and he should benefit from his commitment to the farm).*

Father married Dean to Sally on that cold February day with his nephews and nieces acting as bridesmaids and pageboys. Grandfather agreed to move out of the Farmhouse and to live in one of the cottages on the estate. We all helped our grandparents move out and helped Dean move on. Mostly at weekend or when other members of the family had days off. The whole process took just 3 weeks. During this time of upheaval Dean and Sally lived with our parents. I tried to get back to see our parents at least every two weeks or when I had a day off or two off in midweek. That is an under statement as when you are a journalist for a news agency having time off is seldom guaranteed, you have to take pot luck. Often Von would get frustrated having made all the arrangements to go to Essex from our home in Stanmore, for me chasing around London to cover a breaking story. My relationship with Scotland Yard could have been better. If a story broke that would be of international importance or have an appeal to commonwealth countries I would get a call. They had a series of phone numbers they could call me on and I carried a personal pager. It would bleep and a phone number would be displayed that I had to call. *(Today the mobile phone is more widely used so bleepers are not so common now apart from in hospitals and some schools.)*

After the wedding, we went onto the reception at the White Hart. I had just given my best man speech and sat down when my pager bleeped. I excused myself from the table and asked the landlord at the White Hard if I could use his phone. It was from my immediate boss in Paris he told me a war had broken out in Angola and as the regular guy who covered breaking news in Africa was in hospital I was asked to cover this fracas. I got back to the reception and asked the MC if I could borrow the microphone. "I wish to apologies to everybody but I have to leave this reception for my dear younger brother I have just taken a call from my office in Paris, I am wanted to cover a breaking story in

Angola" I paused "for those who do not know where that is, it is in Africa and I have to leave straight away. My brother Derek was the first to approach me and offered to take on the mantle of best man for the rest of the proceedings. Von put her arm round me. "Don't worry about us Dexter I will stay with my parents with the kids until you get back or you know more when you get there" She paused, kissed me on the lips and whispered "I love you so much Dexter, make sure you come back to me in one piece." I said farewell to the rest of the family and kissed my new sister in law and Dean wished me luck. I reciprocated.

I drove to the London airport parked my car and picked up my ticket that had been ordered and paid for from the Paris office. One hour later, I was sitting on the plane heading for Angola. But we landed in the neighbouring country of Namibia where arrangements had been made for me to travel by road to Angola. Probably the worst travel I could remember over rough terrain for several hours before we entered Angola. Local informers and one other journalist brought me up to date with this breakout of hostilities. I was relieved from my duties three days later by an African guy who lived in the neighbouring state of the Congo. In a war zone I almost got shot by sniper but for the quick thinking of my guide who pulled me to the ground and saved my life. This was to be my first overseas assignment one of many over the next 44 years.

(The Portuguese Colonial War (Portuguese: Guerra Colonial), also known as the Overseas War in Portugal (Portoguese: Guerra do Ultramar) or in the former colonies as the War of liberation (Portoguese: Guerra de Libertaçá), was fought between Portugal's military and the emerging nationalist movements in Portugal's African colonies from February 1961 to 1971).

When I arrived at Heathrow airport, the first thing I did was phone my wife I had not done so from Africa. I had tried several times but the line would not connect. I had however been able to phone my report to my agency office in Pretoria in South Africa. When Von heard my voice,

I could hear her excitement. I apologised that I could not phone before. She accepted my apology. It was the first time in our life together that I had not spoken to her every day. Von must have sensed I was arriving at her parents' home for before I drove up the drive the door was open and there she was with Aqyza and Linda by her side running out to meet me. Our lips locked together and our kids holding onto me putting their arms around my legs. Connie and George were both pleased to see their son-in-law. The kettle was on and good old English food spread on the table. I had eaten abroad but certainly not English cuisine, and that is what I missed. After the meal, I helped Von put our offspring to bed and they listened intently as I told them a bedtime story. I departed from their room only when they fell asleep. Arm in arm, Von and I leaving their room, went to our bedroom and I made up for my lack of romance and sexual activity. I was as randy as hell, I had missed what I had been used too since our marriage. I can remember what Von said "Dexter you are so hot and your prowess now was better than ever before", she laughed and concluded "You should abstain more often and be as good as this", I was feeling so energetic that once was not enough and that night I penetrated my wife 3 times. She did not object and if I had wanted more, I know she would have obliged. It was good to be home and in bed with my beloved.

We bade farewell to George and Connie in the morning and headed back home to Stanmore. I toyed with the idea of telling her about my close brush with death. I decided against it for the time being, anyway the kids were in the back and I did not want them to know how close their father came to being terminated.

That evening I had a call from Mr. Davis, my boss. He was pleased with my report and asked me if I was willing to take On the role of substitute journalist. This would mean I would act as cover for any of the agency journalists when they were on leave or off sick. It would mean I could go anywhere in the world. I talked this over with Von, at first she was apprehensive but I reassured her that it would only mean at the maximum two weeks away and anyway Mr. Davis had explained if the country was on the safe list I could take my wife with me. Of course, I would have to talk this over with Von's parents to see if they would have their grandchildren if Von came with me. After about an hour, I eventually got my wives acceptance. I phone Peter Davis and told him I would accept this position, after I had phoned George and Connie who said they would be happy to baby-sit their grandchildren.

Chapter 9

TEMPTED WITHOUT RESISTANCE

I was to continue as the London correspondent for the agency until April when the new person to cover London was introduced to me. She was 19 just out of college and as eager as a beaver to get started. Sue Taylor was her name and she was a very beautiful looking 6-foot blonde with mesmerizing blue eyes pert nose and an ample figure with a smile enough to raise any man's blood pressure and date I say a sexual tease. It was just as well Von was not with me otherwise Sue and her obvious flirting with me would have provoked Von to have words with her on worse puncher her lights out. I perhaps being under her spell accepted having coffee with her at the Lyons teahouse in Marble Arch. I was duty bound to bring her up to date on contacts in London for references to being informed of newsworthy information.

She lived in Kingsbury, just four stops before my station at Stanmore. I am not proud of myself for my indiscretion. I should have had more self-control. Her flat was above the newsagents in the High Street just a few minutes from the station. As the train pulled into Kingsbury Station, I was about to say goodbye to her when she grabbed my hand and led me off the train "Come on back to my place and tell me more about your life" She insisted. Like a lamb under her spell, I allowed her to take me up to her flat. It was not a flat as such but what we call now days a studio flat. Prominent in the middle of her apartment was a large double bed a separate kitchen and bathroom come toilet.

Sue perched herself on the bed and patted the bed beside her. I found myself subject to her will and then her lips were on mine her hand expertly removing my jacket and tie before undoing the buttons on my shirt and stealth-fully undoing my flies and grasping my manhood. She quickly dispensed of all her clothing until she was kneeling in front of me just wearing her earrings. She pulled down my trousers and underpants to my ankles and buried her head into my groin. It was clear to me then she was a genuine golden blonde as the hair round her pubes provided that proof. After this ex marital indiscretion, she commented "I know you are a married man, so I won't let you fuck me, anyway I don't suppose you carry rubbers in your wallet". I gulped "No, I don't use them now." I dressed as she went into the kitchen and put the kettle on "you will have a cup of tea before you go" I nodded my head, but I was surprised by what I had let Sue do to me. We drank our tea in comparative silence after what seemed a very long pause she spoke. "I'm not one much for fucking guys but I do love to suck a good cock and if you like we can do it again sometime". I was too shocked to refuse but uttered the words "OK but I best being going now Von will have our tea on."

I caught the train back to Stanmore tube station and as I sat in the carriage I was having conflicting feelings about my unexpected sexual experience with Sue. One part of me had enjoyed it without shame whilst probably my more true self was disgusted. I loved Von and if she ever found out about my unfaithfulness, albeit a one off, she would be more upset of that I was sure and maybe she would want me out of her life. The very thought of that kept playing on my mind. It was almost our 4th wedding anniversary and I had allowed myself to be tempted without resistance into an extra marital affair but I tried to justify my actions that I had not gone looking for it. It found me and I was found wanting in not resisting the temptation. I uttered to myself a prayer "Good Lord please forgive me and save Yvonne from ever knowing about my adultery amen".

I tried to behave normally when I got home to my family and our normal kiss was as usual as it always was. It was getting late and the kids were just in bed so I told them a bed-time story whilst Von hovered near the door her hand on the lentil. She was watching me carry out my fatherly task. As my two angels drifted off to sleep I thanked God for the gift of children and stood up. Von came up to me and sniffed "What is that smell on you, that is strong perfume" I had to think quickly "You know I was meeting my successor as the London correspondent and that's her perfume you are smelling, probably when she said goodbye and kissed me on the cheek" Von never queried my explanation and snuggled up to me as we went downstairs to watch some television before retiring to bed. I was not found wanting in that department in relation to romance and making love before we both fell asleep.

A few days later, I got confirmation of my appointment with the new agency. The Peter Davis agency had joined forces with another news agency is also in Australia and the new name would be Oceania Media News Agency (OMNA). It was on the same day I got a call telling me that I was assigned to South Africa for two weeks. It has to be said that due to the apartheid in that country I would not be able to take my wife. Strict rules forbid white people in from, romantic liaisons with other than those of the same race.

I kissed Von and my children goodbye at the airport, and she would drive the car home. It was only our second fresh car as the A30 had been a good friend and reliable workhorse for just over 3 years. The replacement was a 1959 Ford Consul just 18 months old. Von and myself shared. *(It was an ideal size for our family and apart from the extra horsepower it had much more room, and the colour blue and 3 gears on the steering wheel, as opposed to a 4 gear shift on the floor in the Austin A30 and separate seats the consul had a bench seat so if need be we could get three people in the front and the same in the back.)*

I arrived in Pretoria, the capital of South Africa just as the sun was sinking. I hired a cab to take me to the guest house the Crimea was just a few miles from the airport. I was fully aware or so I thought of the race relation rules of this country. I was not happy with them but I had to try and live with that situation.

A few days later after attending the Parliament I was walking home and on the opposite side of the road where the black people walked, I recognised an old RAF buddy Francis Mason. I called out his name and he saw me. I crossed the road and gave him a hug. We were about to start a conversation when 4 burly policemen appeared on the scene, 2 blacks and 2 whites. They pulled us apart. I protested but they took no notice saying I had broken the law by fraternizing with a person of a different colour and race. I was taken to an interview room where I was interrogated.

Despite checking my credentials and being aware, I was a British journalist they still left me alone in the room whilst they departed with my confiscated documents. After what seemed like an age an older police officer in civilian clothes sporting a recently shaven head and a deep scar down the side of his face came into the room. I stood up but he told me "Sit down Mister Barren, we checked you out, you are who you say you are, but I must warn you, you are not in England, now you are in South Africa and you obey our rules." He paused spat onto the floor then he peered threateningly into my face just a few inches from eyes. "You do not fraternize in public places with the blacks, the cape coloureds, the Indians or the chinks in this country, only white people if you understand that you are free to go" he informed me and haded me back my documents. He opened the door and in a gruff voice "OK get out and don't let me see you in here again or if you break our laws again you will go to prison". "Can you tell me what will happen to my friend" I asked. "Niggers are not your friends in this country." He grunted and pushed me towards the reception are of the police stations. I saw Francis walking out of the station and unseen by the police when outside slipped in his hand the address I was saying at. He smiled briefly and hurried away.

I got talking with the owner of the guest house, he seemed a nice guy and I told him what had happened to me down town. He explained that what I did was against the law by touching him in public. However, so long as I did not touch a black person in public there was not a problem.

Later that evening in private, I met up with Francis, and we exchanged each other's history since we had both been demobbed from the RAF. In the police station, he was subjected to an hour's detention like myself before he was released with a similar warning to me about fraternizing in public.

I was not happy being in South Africa as I was opposed to a regime that did not respect all people as equal. In England, in the early 50's there had been some racial conflict to the immigrants from the Caribbean, but they were not segregated as they were in South Africa. Separate hotels, buses, benches, restaurants, toilets and places of worship and on the trains separate carriages etc.

I walked into a church in down town Pretoria and the only person I could see there was a black boy in his early teens on his knees facing the cross with his hands clasped together in front of him, obviously praying to our God. As got close to him the priest walked up to him lifting him up from the floor and screaming at him "You don't pray in this church go to your own down the road. He then kicked him up his backside that sent him sprawling to the ground. The boy got up and ran out of the church pushing past me as he went. I was angry that a man of God should stop anybody from praying. The priest saw me and smiled "Sorry about that sir, we can't let niggers pray in our church, they got their own places of worship". My fist answered him right between the eyes and he slumped to the floor and fully unconscious. To me, that was justified anger and the first time I had ever hit a priest or anybody in a church. I quickly made my exit out of a side entrance. Nobody saw me. And two days later, I was on my way back to the London. I did read a short three-line report on the attack on the priest, which was slightly inaccurate in the fact it described the assailant as a black youth. More lies it seemed as the report stated the priest was kicked in the head and body several times and needed medical attention. With an overnight stay in hospital. I wondered if perhaps the black boy came back and inflicted the addicitonal injuries to this priest. Whatever he got was deserved, as his attitude towards a person praying to God was not the actions of a true Christian priest. I felt no remorse for my actions. Nobody should be stopped from praying to God, regardless of colour or race. We are all equal in the eyes of God. I was reminded of Shylock the Jew in Shakespeare's play the merchant of Venice.

(Hath not a Jew eyes? Hath not a Jew hands, organs, dimensions, sense, affections, passions; fed with the same food, hurt with the same weapons, subject to the same diseased, healed by the same means, warmed and cooled by the same winter and summer as a Christian is? If you prick us, do we not bleed? If you tickle us, do we not laugh? If you poison us, do we not die?

And if you wrong us, shall we not revenge? If we are like you in the rest, we will resemble you in that. If a Jew wrong a Christian, what is his humility? Revenge. If a Christian wrongs a Jew, what should his sufferance be by Christian example? Why, revenge.) The same is true of any human being.

Chapter 10

MY GRANDFATHER AND FATHER CALLED HOME

I spent several hours relating to Von about my experiences in South Africa. She was just as appalled as I was about the racial divisions in South Africa, and agreed that I should not accept another position there in the future whilst the country was adopting their policy of apartheid. I would be honest in my retelling of the situation in that country to Von's parents, my own as well as to my grandparents and other family members. In unison, they agreed that this country had a wicked attitude towards humanity. A serious blot on the face of God's earth. As a family, we prayed that in the future the country would see the blinding errors in the continuation of their policy of segregation. *(In 1994 apartheid in South Africa came to a close when the former jailed leader Nelson Mandela became President of a free South Africa.)* Our prayers were answered.

Over the next few years, I found myself visiting several countries as relief reporter. Only a few days after returning from my second trip to Africa as a correspondent. I was asked to go to Norway for 9 days. Von accompanied me on this trip and enjoyed the experience of being in this country where during the period there we saw no darkness aptly called the land of the midnight sun. She met and conversed with a few Philippine ladies married to Norwegians. Von's grasp of the native tongue of the Philippines had improved, thanks largely to her mother and of course myself. She grasped the opportunity of being able to converse in this language of her mother. We both found these Nordic people to be very friendly and there was a lack of racism.

My next trip abroad saw us both embark to Brazil. Von did not feel comfortable there as a strong hint of prejudiced against the street children when we found out were often shot as being surplus to requirements. Culled as often occurs in some countries for an access of animals. As she was deeply unhappy with the situation regarding these children she could not bear to stay in a moment longer than was absolutely necessary. My tour there was to last a month, and Von stayed only 5 days before she flew home.

When I was in a hotel on my own, a Brazilian lady wanted to attach herself to me. I enjoyed the conversation with her as we talked a lot about football. When she talked about coming up to my room, I realized that a visit to my room would possible end in a compromising situation. Her body close and as I leaned back my head came in contact with a naked leg. I abruptly opened my eyes and looked to see that the owner of the leg was Maria. She was on my bed totally naked. Her brown body glisten in the sunlight highlighted by the fact she was covered in oil. I leapt off the bed as she embarked from the bed herself and before I had time to fasten my towel, she had stolen it from where I had left it and threw it towards the bathroom. She moved towards me and I was under her spell. As she threw her arms around me pulling my body towards her own. I am only a human of the male gender and heterosexual. Could I possibly resist this brown eyed angel with her pulsating smooth ebony skin clinging to my own uncovered and fully exposed body in the throes of a growing excitement in my nether region. I wanted to hold on to this enticing female as my sex brushed rigid against the hairs between the top of her legs. If I closed my eyes, I could imagine this body being my wife Von. She now kneeling in front of me and doing exactly as Sue Taylor did to me in her Kingsbury flat. Maria was in control and I could not find the will or the energy to push her away. The climax came just a few seconds before the knock on my door and Maria pulled away from me and vanished into the bathroom. I pulled my robe on and standing inside the door, I called out "who is it" "A gentleman in the lobby sir to see you urgently" came to reply. I hastily dressed in casual dark trousers and white shirt. Maria emerged from the bathroom and quickly dressed in her clothes. She kissed me full on the lips and spoke the words "I come back to finish what we started" I never uttered a word as she departed from my room.

Downstairs in the lobby, Mr. Gonzales met me from the

local newspaper. He informed me about a demonstration to be held outside the government building. Of course, I was interested, I would be failing in my duty as a journalist if I did not report on this demo.

Maria did not come back to my hotel room again, although I did see her in the Hotel bar with another man. It was an incident of one off and though part of me wanted a further encounter with her delightful body and mouth, my moral side was urging restraint. I did console myself with the important fact on the only two occasions my body had been subjected to carnal intrusion with other than my wife, it was only the mouth to my appendage and not full sexual intercourse.

I did a full a report on the Demo and faxed this to the agency in Australia. It was to be my last major report other than a few less important communications I forwarded to ONMA from Brazil.

I arrived home to be met by Von at the airport and our now habitually lingering kiss sealed our reunion as well as making up for two weeks without the taste of her mouth on mine. The children were eager to see me too as it had been a month since I had held them in my arms or told them a bedtime story. The wanted to know along with Von all that I had experienced in Brazil and I tried to make it as interesting as I could obviously I omitted my liaison with Maria and the diabolical uncivilized way they disposed of the street children.

Three days I was off to Mexico to 3 weeks then without a break I was on my way to India for a further two weeks, followed by a week in Australia. Von was able to join me and we more than made up for my absence from her bed for 5 weeks.

The occasion for me being in Perth Western Australia was to meet with the new directors of ONMA. The death of Peter Davis had resulted in his daughter Iris becoming my new boss. She was 45 and though married, she was going through a rather messy divorce in that year of 1962. She was in admiration of my own marriage and promised that she would not let me be absent from my wife for more than 3 weeks at a time if it were humanly possible. Part of the reason for our weeks long stay in Perth was for me to pick up my first award as ONMA journalist of the year for 1961. I felt humbled as the premier of Western Australia presented the prestigious award to me.

Later in 1962, I went to Brisbane Sydney Melbourne, Darwin Adelaide and Canberra in Austria with a 3-week visit to cover a number of cricket games and other activities. Von joined me for the entire trip. Our kids were calling us the jet setters. Of course, they were pleased to see us, as were George and Connie. They made a few trips to our house inn Elstree that we still rented. A decision had soon to be made about us making up our minds if we would purchase a house in Hertfordshire or Essex. Whatever our decision, George was soon to retire and had accepted several offers for his bakery in Castle Hedingham. He and Connie would remain in the house in Halstead and make frequent visits to our house in Elstree, even if Von and I were away together.

It was in 1963, just after our family Christmas at our parent's homes that tragedy struck. Grandfather died and his funeral took pace in Hempstead and burial in nearby Wimbish, not far from Saffron Walden. Having just recovered from grandfather's death in December, tragic news again when my father was called home after suffering a massive heart attack I February 1961. I flew home from Vancouver just 24 hours after arriving in Canada. Father was buried in Halstead and over 300 people attended his funeral and thanksgiving service. The wake was held in The Bull Inn near where the Halstead station used to be located before the closure of the railway in 1962 by Doctor Beaching.

I flew back to Canada the day after the funeral and chanced a meeting with Sandy, a lady reporter from the USA in Vancouver and her Language was evidently somewhat provocative. Even at the table we sat at her hand kept touching mine and I noticed that she had opened her blouse by undoing the first two buttons to reveal more than a glimpse of her cleavage. As she leaned forward to brush an insect off my shoulder, I could clearly see the nipples on her breasts. The bra she wore was obviously a little too big for her and I could see without any restriction what I could sample if I were to give in to temptation. True it had been 2 days since I left England and I was feeling horny. My mind flashed back to my romantic liaison with Sue Taylor in her Kingsbury flat and Maria in Brazil. I had given into temptation twice, although I did not have intercourse but the pleasure of those ladies on my mouth and my sex I could not resist. All the signs were there that this lady wanted me. Should I give in and satisfy my carnal desire, Von was not here and surely I would only be a salve to my sexual requirements, but no diverting my love for Von. I paused in thought as I could visualize her laid out on my bed, legs apart and pulling me onto her body. At that precise moment as Sandy again leaned forward and planter her lips on mine forcing her tongue into my mouth. A picture of Von manifested itself in my brain. Seeing her beauty and my two children by her side helped my temptation to dwindle. I declined the offer to bring her to my room. I left her seated by the table and obviously in disappointment.

I lay on my bed my head still with vision of my wife as she left me at the airport just 2 days ago. The long lingering kiss and waving each other goodbye as she went into the departure lounge. IU put all thoughts of Sandy out of my minds as I decided to take a shower.

I emerged from the shower walking naked into be my bedroom drying my hair with my towel. My eyes were looking towards the window as the bright sunshine filled the room I looked away as I squinted my eyelids to cover my pupils from this array brilliance. I sat on the bed, my eyelids still shut as I leaned back my head came in contact with a naked leg. I abruptly opened my eyes and looked to see that the owner of the leg was Sandy. She was on my bed totally naked. Her body glisten in the sunlight highlighted by the fact she was covered in oil. I leapt off the bed as she embarked from the bed herself and before I had time get my towel she moved towards me and I was under her spell. As she threw her arms round me pulling my body towards her own. This was uncanny, it was the same scenario as in

Brazil. Could I possibly resist this temptation as in Brazil? Sandy was clinging to my own uncovered and fully exposed body with excitement in my groin. I wanted to hold on to this enticing female as my sex brushed against my pubic hair. I closed my eyes and imagined this body being my wife Von. Sandy was kneeling in front of me and doing exactly as Sue and Maria had done.

Chapter 11

YOU ARE NOT MY SLAVE

Over the next few years, I was to visit in access of a 100 countries. Some I visited were routine and most boring with nothing to really trigger my memory. My first visit to Ghana was in 1964 and following instructions from ONMA spouses could only be taken on assignments in class. A classified countries deemed as safe, but to a maximum of 28 days either as 2 periods of 14 days or one period of 28 days. Although Ghana was a class A destination, Von decided to stay at home in Elstree.

My assignment in Ghana was on behalf of the United Nations. It was my job to stay in Tema 16 miles from the capital Accra. My task was to monitor ship movements into the docks and their cargo. This meant that apart from visiting the docks every day I could also observe from my condo on the beach the movements of these ships. The reason for this observation was not told to me. Every hour of the day I had to observe any movements and the name of the ship going into the harbor. I shared this task with another person, a resident of Ghana called Adabo Taylor, he would monitor at night and myself by day. All information I gathered, I would pass onto Adabo and he in turn would forward this information on to the UN.

This stay in Ghana I assumed would be boring and for much of the time it was. I had been assigned a native girl of 18 called Precious who would look after me clean the condo and cook food for me etc., She was a very sweet ebony girl at just under five foot and slim, who always seemed to have a smile. Mostly she was dressed in either a coloured one-piece dress down below the knees or a white dress just above the knees.

She was always on time at 9 am in the morning. She would clean the condo make my bed, undertake my washing and bring me food that she would cook. It was very basic food mostly of African cuisine, but she did on a few occasions was able to bring me some English food.

I was bored most of the time. It was as well I had my radio with me including plenty of reading material. The beach was mostly deserted and was able to swim without need of any bathers. This seemed to be my only way to stem off total boredom.

I had been in Ghana for 5 days and it was on this first Saturday morning that Precious came to carry out her normal duties. Normally, I would not bother to wear clothes from 6 am to 9 am as I had a light breakfast after a quick swim, and completed my report on the portable typewriter. She was in a cheerful mood for her three-hour stint at my condo. "I will be in earlier tomorrow as I want to go to church" she informed me. "That's fine Precious, I would like to go to church too, I will join you if that is OK with you". "Yes, we have white people come to our church too." She informed me as she set about her tasks after she made me a cup of tea and egg with bacon in 2 slices bread. She was a cheerful person and I loved talking to her and teaching me a few words of her native tongue, although she spoke good English.

I had risen at my normal time of 6 am and had forgotten that Precious was coming early. In fact, I had forgotten to ask her what time she would be coming, I went for a quick swim and without a care in the world returned to the condo wearing nothing. I sat down at the table with the window in front of me and began typing out my report. I did not hear Precious enter the condo and was only aware of her presence when she walked up to me and said "Good morning Dexter" I was started and immediately covered my privates with my hands. "Am sorry you see me like this. If you wait I will go get myself dressed." "No need Dexter, the man before you, he not dress much of the time here, I see him naked I not worry" She smiled "I cleared my throat "If you prefer me to dress I will do so"

"Please no need Mr. Dexter, this is your home now, you be as you want to be" she suggested. I felt less embarrassed at her comment. She then surprised me by saying "If you want, I too can be naked" I looked at her directly after turning my chair round. "Precious, it's not what I want. It's what you want. You are not my slave; I cannot order you to do that" she smiled. "I want if you not object for me to be naked" "OK!" I exclaimed. I have no objections, if it's what you want." Without any further reply, she pulled the white dress over her head to reveal her total nudity. She then went into the kitchen and cooked my breakfast whilst I continued to complete my report.

I had to admire her slim young body as she returned and as I stared at her she commented "You like my body; I like yours" A big grin was visible on her face as she gently rubbed my hairy chest. "I love your hair on your so white body" she looked down at my limp appendage and pointed at it "it not as big as the man here before you, white men not have big ones" I laughed. "The man before me must have been very big then" I remarked. A broad grin spread across her face and she laughed. "Sometimes it got very big" she held her hands out about 12 inches apart. I raised my eyebrows and blurted out. "How did it get that big?" Precious held her hand out and explained "With these I make it big, I can make yours big too if you want me to".

She sat her bottom on the back of her legs and took my cock into her hands and began to rub it furiously. It was only sex after all so as long as she did not want me to seduce here, I let her bring my cock to its full size "You like me to suck it Mr. Dexter?" She asked as she looked up at me with those piercing brown eyes. I said nothing and let her do as she desired.

Over the remaining three weeks, it seemed to her, a must do duty she must perform, as she always asked "Mr. Dexter, you like me make you big?" I never had the heart to refuse or was it my sexual desire to let her do what she requested to do. Although she would always rub her own sex top and bottom, she never did ask me to seduce here, and I never did kiss her on the lips, only on the cheeks.

I had to admit that I did miss this ritual from Precious when I returned home to England. Of course with my wife Von, we enjoyed the full requirements of sex from foreplay to seduction. I did not feel guilty as I felt that what I did with Precious was not love just sex.

The children grew up so quickly and attended school in Borehamwood, Von even got herself a part time job at a local solicitors. George and Connie came to see Von and the kids at least every other week. The bakery now sold, George had more time on his hands. My widowed mother would visit when I was back in the UK.

I was home for only four days when I got a call from Iris Davis of ONMA herself. She thanked me for my dedication to the UN initiative in Ghana. I asked what was the reasoning behind this job I had been employed to do. Dexter my dear, if I knew I would tell you, but alas I was not privy to why only that it was of importance to the security of Africa, and ultimately the world" She paused I want you to go to Columbia," she continued. "Is that Washington district of Columbia" I exclaimed excitedly. I heard Iris take a deep breath for continuing" "Alas no Dexter, it is the country of Columbia, not a class A for security, but I know you will be careful". I felt she sensed my disappointment of my anticipation of going to the USA for the first time in my life.

I was to fly to Bogata, the capital of Columbia (not to be confused with British Columbia, a district in Canada) *(The Republic of Columbia (Spanish: República de Colombia), is a country in northwestern South America. It's bordered to the east by Venezuela and Brazil, to the south by Ecuador and Peru, to the North by the Atlantic Ocean and to the west by Panama and the Pacific Ocean).* At this time that I went to Columbia, it was a country that was very deep into the growing and distribution of hard illicit and illegal drugs, I would have to be very cautious. I had no love of drugs as in later life, I was to see the damage it done to many young people and those not so young. I recommend a good book on the subject 'NO ROOM FOR JUGGLERS IN MY CIRCUS' by Jason Cook.

Chapter 12

DRAGGED FROM THE CAR

I was given a good description of my contact in Columbia, I meet him outside the airport main entrance. He was Randolph King an American living in Columbia and attached to the American consulate. A tall black heavy built Negro in his late 40's with a shaved head. He was standing by the side of a black sedan smoking a very large cigar "Hello Dexter pleased to meet you." He extended his hand and I felt his strong grip on my fingers. We got in the car and we drove away from the airport before heading out into the country to his home where I was to stay with his family.

"So you married a lady from the Asia so Miss Davis told me" was his comment. "Well not quite her mother was from the Philippines but her father was English and she was born in the UK" I responded. Well Dexter, I had been married for 24 years, 22 when I got married to my Columbian wife and we have two gorgeous daughters, Alice 23 and Andrea 21". He paused and continued "I guess you got kids too Dexter, or you just got married". I informed him of my young family and he nodded his approval adding. "How does your wife take to it you being away so much" Von has got used to it now, we been married over 6 years now". I informed him. He glanced in the internal mirror and commented "That car behind us has been following us ever since we left the airport. I get kinder worried when I get followed, so I am going to increase speed and shake him off." Rand as I was to call him slammed his foot down and we more e than doubled the speed of his car in a matter of seconds. The car that had been following us was still on our tail. Randy swung the wheel hard to the left with amazing skill and we started going up and unmade road through a wooded area. I looked back and saw the rogue car was no longer behind us. Randy pulled off the road and parked the sedan out of view, as he was certain that the rouge car would have turned round and in pursuit of us again. He was right we watched this car bump along this rough road and out of sight. We waited a few minutes before Randy pulled the car back onto the rough terrain and we headed back to the main road.

It was unfortunate, we had only gone a few yards when his front tire burst and we hit a tree. The force of the impact threw us both forward. I gained consciousness just as two armed men with black ski masks covering their faces dragged me from the car and put a blindfold over my eyes. They left Randy where he was. It looked as if he had been shot as the front of his shirt was covered in blood. I was pushed into their car. I heard one of the men speaking in Spanish saying "He is dead is the other guy no good taking him" The other kidnapper agreed by nodding his head.

We arrived at a building in what I took to be in no less than a few minutes. Once inside, they removed my blindfold, took my watch, passport, press card, wallet the loose change in my pocket and pushed me into a room with four other people. Three men of about thirty and a girl probably in her early twenties. All were white. The kidnappers slammed the door and I could hear bolts being closed.

We introduced ourselves. Bob an American, Philip from New Zealand. Terry from my own country and Amanda also from the UK. They were all journalist, or so they told me. They had been snatched from their car they were all traveling in the same car apart from Amanda who was grabbed whilst walking in the street. They had been captive for just 4 hours when I joined them. We assumed we were being held captive for a ransom.

Six hours after I had been kidnapped, food was brought into us just a basic meal of bread and something that looked like meat, and tasted like a mixture of fish and pork. We ate it as we were hungry and they gave us only water to drink. My fellow prisoners had not eaten for over 10 hours. They attacked the food ravenously.

It was perhaps 2 days later that we heard the commotion outside our cell and several gunshots before there was a moment of silence. It was soon broken when we were aware of the bolts on the door being opened, we were all terrified were we the next to be shot. A sigh of relief as the door swung open we saw six armed American soldiers standing there. They hurried us out of the building and into a waiting truck. We were free. Imagine my surprise to find that in the truck was Randy no blood on his shirt and only a bandage on his head where he had struck the windscreen. It is a remarkable story and I have to let Randy tell it.

RANDY'S STORY

"After the car crashed into the tree, I gained consciousness and saw the rouge car approaching. I realized this was going to be a kidnapping, I emptied the contents of a tomato sauce bottle onto my shirt to give them the impression I was dead. It worked and the soon as they drove away with you Dexter, I got out of the car and walked back to the main road. I got a lift and went straight to a phone box and called the consulate. The came out to me within a couple of hours. We returned to my sedan change the tire and I was able to drive it back to the garage. We got your bags out of the car and called in Becky the dog. She was able to sniff your clothes and get a lead. We went back to where the car hit the tree and Becky did the rest. We saw where you were being held but we could not risk going in at that stage since we were only lightly armed. We called the States and then sent in a special commando unit. The rest you know.

BACK TO MY STORY

I spent the next few weeks at Randy's home and his family made me really welcome. Randy had to go away for five days on what he referred to as a special assignment. I was to keep in touch with The American Consulate from where I was to obtain any newsworthy leads. Andrea the youngest daughter was a real, dare I say sex siren. She revealed all the signals that she wanted to bed me.

I met my fellow captives a few days after our release and enjoyed a beer in a local tavern sharing stories in their pasts and up to date with other local breaking news. My report on the capture had been sent to ONMA and the following day many newspapers in Bogata carried the full story. One variation was it stated that Colombian soldiers rescued us. This was because relations between the USA and Columbia were fragile. If it had been known that American commandos had been into this sovereign country without prior invitation, all hell would have broken loose within diplomatic circles.

Bonita king, Randy's wife was a woman of high intelligence and trusted me in the house alone with her two daughters. She was called away urgently to be of service to a sick relative, her sister Katrina had fallen down the stairs and had broken both arms and requested help that only another woman could provide. She had four boys that could not provide the personal touches that a woman would be required to administer, given the complication of her injuries. If you don't understand what I mean, I am sorry I cannot elaborate any further.

When I returned to their house that evening. Alice had gone out leaving Andrea alone. At first when I entered the home, I could not see or hear anybody in the house and assumes that I was alone. I went to the freezer and took out a couple of eggs and bread intending to make myself a meal. I was just about to put the eggs in the frying pan when Andrea centered the kitchen wearing only a towel. "No you not need to cook Dexter, I made you a stew that is in the oven" she explained as she opened the oven with e sides of her towel which remained attached to her body. Well it goes without saying as she lifted this dish of stew from the oven her towel was raised. And as she walked towards the table where I was sitting I had a clear view of her bush under the towel. This longhaired ebony beauty was making my libido race. I was tempted to grab her leg, as it was poised near my hand as she put the dish on the table. "You and I can share this" she smiled. That precise moment her towel fell downwards and finished up on the floor. She made no attempt to stop it from falling and made no haste as she re-attached it to her body. Deliberately taking her time as if no tease me. Without warning or by your leave she leaned over and planted a big wet kiss on my lips and once more her towel was parted from her body. Her hand was down on my flies and she was feeling that I was aroused.

Alice was coming into the house and Andrea departed quickly leaving me in a frustrated state. Oh so pleased that Von was not here to witness this incident. I had never considered myself to be a sex symbol to women but it seemed I was. I had to learn self-control, but God knows I am only human, and why is he giving me all this temptation or perhaps it is the devil responsible.

Andrea returned to the kitchen come diner a few minutes later dressed in jeans and a white T-shirt. All three of us tucked into the stew. We made pleasant conversation as a threesome but I was wary that these two girls wanted more than just a conversation. It was just the questions seemed to have double meanings or leading innuendos. We watched a television, seated on the sofa together by invitation both girls shifted apart on the large family size settee and asked me to site between them.

I did tell you earlier that Columbia was heavily into drugs, but I never expected Randy's daughters to be involved. How did I know? Let me tell you. I accepted a drink from them, not suspecting that anything was out of the ordinary. My head began to buzz a little was I hallucinating, I was aware of both girls undressing me. I was paralysed, unable to resist.

I was an unwilling participant in their little game. They had all my clothes off in what seemed a few seconds and then they both stripped themselves and each of them was kissing my body. They were manipulating me to their will. Both went down to my now rampant organ. I was aware of two mouths sharing it alternatively. Alice then sat on my mouth and my tongue came out of my mouth to enter her heaven. I was partially conscious when I was helped upstairs to one of the bedrooms. They both continued to abuse my body. Sucking, licking. They forced me to insert my organ into their heavens but I was powerless to offer any resistance.

I awoke that morning painfully aware that both girls physically abused my body. My now limp organ was sore there were bite marks on my body (love bites). I was feeling drained but not feeling satisfied as my head was spinning. I asked Andrea to phone the consulate to say I would not be in as I was not well. Andrea looked at me in a remorseful way and remarked. "I think we went too far with you, we are sorry."

In a way I was pleased that there were no duplications of that abuse. However, I must not lie I did once more have carnal knowledge with Andrea. It was just before her mother came home and it was only Andrea and myself in the house. I was already in the house and dressed in a pair of shorts, a loose t-shirt and bare feet and lying upon on the settee watching the TV. She came in looked at me and blew me a kiss before she went to take a shower. About 15 minutes later, she returned wearing just a towel. She pushed my feet down off the settee and sat down herself. She purposely opened her tower to give me a full-unhindered view of her assets. "I feel so hot" she explained. "Hope you don't mind if I take this towel off." She concluded. Even though I did not answer she pulled the towel away from her body throwing it over my face. I pulled it off and threw it behind the settee. She was tempting me as she clasped her hands around her ample proportions and tweaked her nipples, before running her hand down to the lips of her sex. It was too much for a hot bloodied man like myself. Resistance was futile and I soon found myself naked courtesy of the hands of Andrea. I let her mouth find my organ. In the manipulation of our bodies into a more comfortable position, we embarked on a 69 (my mouth to her sex and her mouth to mine). I was thinking of Von as eventually our sexual components came together. I was to climax within a few minutes, and Andrea unlike my wife shouted out a number of obscenities as she herself reached her climax. Thankfully Andrea had informed me that was fitted with a device that prevented pregnancy. I dread to think if I had been the father of a Cambodian child and not to know about it.

I almost had decisive sex with Alice before both Randy and Bonita came back to their house. I was in bed almost asleep when a naked Alice opened my bedroom door and slipper her delicious body in beside mine. She felt for my organ and started to massage it as she pushed her lips against mine. This carnal experience was interrupted by the sound of a car pulling onto the drive and the lights of the car lit up the bedroom. Alice quickly leapt out of bed exclaiming "That's Daddy's car, he is back early".

I never did reveal the secret that both Andrea and Alice had told me never to tell their parents. As if I would, the last thing I wanted was to be confronted with a man twice my size, not that I would feel inferior to him given my martial arts experience.

I never did have any more carnal knowledge in the house with either Alice or Andrea. The only opportunity that was available was down on the beach on a secluded stretch of sand, mile from any prying eyes. It was Saturday and Randy gave his daughters permission to take me sightseeing, he even loaned them the car. We walked around the city for a while before Alice decided that we should go for a swim. We swam naked and fooled around but nothing as strong as sexual intercourse took place.

Randy was sorry to see me go and as he hugged me at the airport, he whispered "pity you are a married man as you would make me a fine son-in-law for either Alice or Andrea". Inwardly, I smiled knowing he did not know what his two daughters and I had shared.

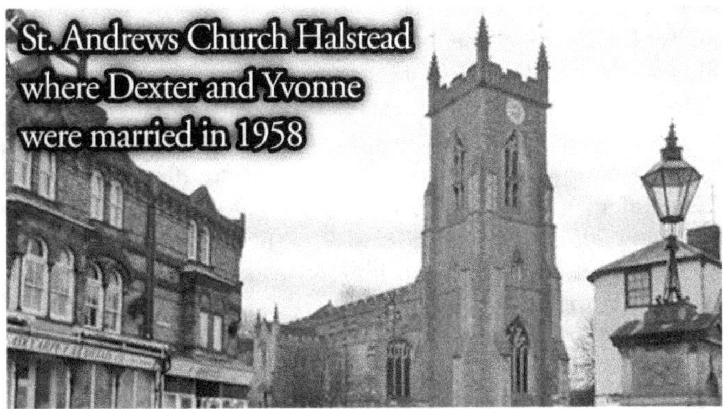

Chapter 13

BACK TO THE UK FOR 6 WEEKS

It was 1970 and I was home for Christmas the first time since 1964. It was time to reflect on the demise of the senior members of our families. Both my grandparents, my father and Von's father.

Christmas was celebrated at our home in Elstree. My mother and Connie had moved to Elstree and together they had purchased a house in the same road as us.

So come the big gathering of the Barren clan and both my brother's my sister and their families came up from their respective homes to our place in Elstree Dean, Sally and their two boys from the farm in Hempsted, Derek, Rosemary and their two boys from their home in Manchester, Denise, Gordon and her son and daughter from their home in Halstead. They had purchased my parents' house in Halstead. Gordon had taken a number of exams in administration and was then the manager of a construction company in Chelmsford. Denise my beloved sister a qualified accountant owning her own accountancy firm in Braintree. Rosemary had gone back to work, as her children were old enough to care for themselves. They both worked in the same hospital in Manchester, Derek now a consultant specializing in heart surgery. Rosemary as head of the gynecologist department. Dean had purchased many additional farms in Hempstead as well as in Great Sampford and Radwinter. Under the umbrella of Barren Estates. He had 40 people working for him all year and this increased to over 100 during the harvest time.

We managed to accommodate all the family in our two homes. Both houses had 4 bedrooms. The kids shared two rooms between them at my Mother's house and my sister's daughter shared with my mother, and Von's mother. Derek and Rosemary had their other room. Dean and Sally slept in Aqyza's room on a guest bed. Denise and Gordon, the same in Linda's room and Gordon's mother with her new husband Frank in the other room.

I looked back on the news items I had covered. The Biafran war, train crash in Argentina, Japanese plane hijacked, Concords maiden flight, Rhodesia breaking off links with the UK, the World Cup in Mexico won by Brazil 4-1 against Italy.

The Christmas party at our house went off well. A few confrontations between the kids, but those arguments were soon sorted out. We all as a family went to the Baptist church in Furze Hill Road, for the traditional Christmas family service. It was such a busy time on Christmas day for the ladies having to cook for the entire family. My brothers and Gordon went to the Wagon and Horses pub after we left the church. This was a 15th century pub built in 1471 located on the Radlett road, the A5 just a mile from main-street in Elstree. Derek opted to drink only soft drinks so the rest of us could drink alcohol without worry of being drunk in charge of a car.

Von and myself retired at just after 1 am and we spent time talking. She surprised me with her line of conversation probably fueled by her communications with other members of my family. "Dexter darling, can I ask you something that is a bit personal?" she began. I held her hand and kissed her lips and I responded. "You know you can ask me anything, we got no secrets and we never have my darling". "I have never asked you to give up your career as a reporter going overseas a lot, but I just wonder when we are not together do you get urges?" she enquired. I took a deep breath, kissed her again and told her in a somewhat manufactured reply. "I do get urges but I use self-control anyway, I always kiss your photo before I go to sleep and again in the morning" "Dexter, I know you do but I wonder that you meet so many people when you are away and girls of course, surely they are attracted to you or they fancy you. She paused sniffed and continued. "When you are at home, you always feel so horny and you want it almost every night, and I wonder how you suppress your horny feelings?" I giggled. "Well, I have my hand and do it whilst I am looking at your photo." Von smiled and sat up in the bed. "So you never been tempted?" she enquired, I lied. "Tempted yes! But, always think of you and take a cold shower so the temptation is cooled." Von put her hands behind her neck, licked her lips provocatively and spoke. "Give me an example of how you were tempted", I decided to add a little truth to my revelations and laying my hand on Von's naked breast (we always slept naked winter and summer). I related some of my temptations. "In Ghana, I was not dressed and Precious, my house girl, came to the Condo early and saw me naked. I told her I would dress but she said I don't have to. So, I didn't then she said, she liked being naked and asked if it was ok if she took her dress off. I did not answer but she took my silence as permission to do so. She had a reasonable nice figure but I never touched her but admired her" Von interrupted "and any more temptations my Dexter?" "In Columbia, Randy and his wife went away and left me alone in the house with his two daughters. One of them walked into the kitchen wearing only a towel that fell off, she stood there totally naked and when I showed no interest she re-fastened her towel and went back to her bedroom to dress", I paused, cleared my throat and continued. "I was in Japan sitting at a table talking with a Japanese female journalist when she lifted up her foot onto my crotch. I removed it straight away. She made some excuse that it was an accident and the incident was forgotten but I knew she had done it on purpose as she had also undone the first three buttons on her blouse that was no accident." Von leaned over to kiss me and her hand went down my chest to lie on my stick of her delight. We made love with all the passion of ecstasy. I was on top of her and she felt happy as we both reached a mutual climax. We then locked our bodies together as we drifted off into sleep.

With Christmas out of the way the family returning to their own home the house seemed extra quiet from 20 people now down to just the four of us. I was able to have a heart to heart with Aqyza and Linda. I asked them what careers they would go for when they reached an age of decision. Of course, it would be their choice. Our son wanted very much to be a journalist, whilst Linda was torn between being a journalist herself or an actress. The later she did enjoy having been in several school plays and went for an audition to be in a television play at the Elstree studios. Unfortunately, she never got the part.

It was inevitable, I would be on my travels again after spending 6 weeks in the UK covering for holidays for the London reporter and East Anglia. I spent a couple of night in Norwich covering a house siege in nearby Stoke Holy Cross. Eventually the man who was holding his wife and baby captive gave himself up after 40 hours. He was taken into custody. Apparently he was suffering from deep depression, lost his job and was about to be evicted from his home. The publicity that came about through TV radio and newspaper coverage prompted local man to cough up the back rent for this family to stay in the house. The father went to a mental institute for treatment. I was to learn later that he was released and found gainful employment with the Good Samaritan who had paid the back rent.

I went to up to Cromer for one night for what turned out to be a dead body washed up on the beach. It was no ordinary person but an Australian politician. He had been on holiday in France with his family and somehow or other his body got washed up on the Cromer beach. This was several miles from France and posed a problem for the local police, as to how he had gotten himself to Cromer. My prompting encouraged the police detective Bill Kerry to order a search off the coast for a boat.

My suggestion was the key to finding an abandoned yacht 7 miles out at sea. It opened another can of worms, as his wife had been on board with him. Yet there was no sign of her. Examination of the boat showed that there had been a struggle on board and the possibility that the Politician had fallen overboard and the wife had probably been kidnapped. This turned out to be the case as the story moved to Scotland where it seemed the kidnappers were holding her for ransom.

I went up to Scotland by train to continue with the story. Changing at Glasgow up to Inverness. I had to change onto another train that took me to Wick on the north coast of Scotland. Having enjoyed the company of several people on the way to Glasgow and then onto Inverness, two of the people from London were travelling to Perth en route to Inverness. I was the only person in the carriage to Inverness and changing onto the Train to Wick, I had a companion. The lady of 26 was called Penny. She was an inch taller than me with a silky cream like texture and flawless smooth skin, deep green eyes, a pert nose, long golden blonde hair, petite tantalizing lips. Slim long legs partly covered by a tartan dress that was a little below the knees and long fur boots. There was no corridor on this train so just as well I had used the toilet facilities at Inverness.

There was nobody on the carriage when I climbed in. In fact, it looked as if I was the only passenger. The snow was coming

down and I hoped it would not delay my journey. The train was just moving off when this lady I spoke of earlier open the door and climbed in. She had trouble closing the door so I helped her to carry out this task.

She introduced herself as Penny a lass from Scotland and on her way home to see her widowed mother. She had been unable to travel up to see her for the new-year celebrations, as she had to work. I politely asked "What job kept you away from your mother?" She smiled as she removed her woolen hat and let her blond curly hair run free after shaking her head. "I am an actress" she replied. What show were you in?" I enquired. "Catch my soul at the Prince of Wales theatre in London" she replied. *(Catch My Soul was based on Shakespeare's play Othello)* I smiled my reply "Alas I am sorry to say I have not seen that play, but I think it was in the states before it came to the UK".

We continued in polite conversation for something with comments about the snow that was still coming down and quite heavy. "I hope the snow does not block the tracks" I exclaimed as I looked out of the window to see the wind jostle the white flakes in the wind. I tempted providence for a few minutes later the train came to an unexpected stop. I wound the window and observed through the flurry than an avalanche of snow was covering the track ahead. Penny came alongside me and observed what I had described. I quickly pulled the window up and sat down opposite Penny. "How long do you think we will be stuck here?" I asked. Penny rubber her chin and pulling her coat collar closer shivered her reply. "It could be hours or days it has happened before 3 years ago and the train was stuck here for 24 hours" "I hope not I did not bring any food with me" I retorted. Penny stood up and took her case down from the rack and took out a selection of sandwiches. "I can share with you when you feel the prangs of hunger, I always come well prepared for emergencies just like this.

We continued our conversation so that we would not been board. She hung on every word I said in respect of my adventures abroad. I even found myself opening up about some of the temptations put in my way by a few ladies. "So why did this girl in Ghana get naked?" she asked. "Yes she did" I replied. "Then what did you do when you were both naked?" "Do you really want to hear that Penny?" I exclaimed. "It's really OK Dexter, I'm very open minded, you can tell me" "what do you think we did" I continued. Penny laughed her response "I guess you fucked her." I resumed my conversation "Not quite but if I told you her mouth went lower than my chest, need I say more". Penny laughed, "So you let her suck your cock, did you like that?" "Well it beats using my hand" I chuckled. A smile stole across Penny's face and she licked her lips provocatively. I waited patiently for her next words sensing that being alone in this carriage would not be restricted to just conversation.

Although it was still snowing outside the atmosphere in the carriage was surprisingly warm. Penny stood up and took of her coat the reveal a hand knitted jumper in cream and green. She lifted this up and revealed her chest with the nipples quite erect. "Do you like this Dexter?" she pouted. My hand went down to my flies and I could feel my appendage growing in statue" No need for an invitation, I think that had been covered in our more than polite conversation that had developed into a sexual flight of the imagination. Her hand dully undid my zip and placing her hand inside my Y fronts she extracted the part of my body she desired, her mouth engulfed it whilst she encouraged me to massage her again exposed breasts. It was fairly warm but too cold to be totally naked. Our sexual foreplay must have heated that carriage up. She stopped before I could climax. She opens her case and took out a large wool blanket pulled the cushions off both sides of the carriage, and then lay them on the floor. She started to remove all her clothes and beckoned me to do the same. I was putty in her hands and yet her earlier manipulation of my cock had warmed me up. I was naked too and we got under the blanket for bodily warmth. Feeling each other's body with mutual masturbation. If she desired intercourse, it was me that curtailed that activity when I explained. "I don't have a condom" Penny replied. "I neither so let's just do each other by hand". We must have been there for a long time as we both fell asleep snuggled up together for warmth. Our bodily heat kept us warm.

We awoke to the sound of the train moving and we quickly dressed and restored the cushions back to the frames. An hour later and some ten hours since we left Inverness, we arrived in Wick. It was not to be the end of our newfound friendship as she invited me to visit her home and meet her mother. At first, her mother thought I was her boyfriend but as she explained, we met on the train and struck a friendship.

My first priority was to meet the Scottish Detective heading the search for the Politicians wife. I found him in the local Police House. It was good news a local ski instructor had noticed that one of the ski lodges was occupied, and he was not aware of anybody booking it. He had with caution crept up to the lodge and saw a lady tied up. On further investigation, he saw no other person in the lodge. He opened the door and untied the lady who it turned out to be the Australian politician's wife. The Ski Instructor used his short wave radio to contact mountain rescue who us turn contacted the local police. A rescue helicopter had then been used to bring the lady back to the civilization of Wick. A search for the kidnappers was begun and two bodies were found close to the ski lodge. The politician's wife identified them as her captors.

The full story I sent to the ONMA also included the incident on board the boat when Sam Jarvis MP tried to overpower the assailants and fell overboard. They tied her up and took her onto their yacht and set off for Scotland. Any more details as to why they took her to Scotland and the reason for the kidnapping would never be found out since both men had perished in the avalanche.

I managed to telex my report to ONMA and accepted an earlier invitation to stay at Penny's Mother's home. If you have never tasted Scottish hospitality you are missing out on one of life's luxuries. A big plateful of lamb stew awaited me with an abundance of local vegetables harvested in the autumn and stored for the winter. This was preceded by haggis soup and for sweet a suet pudding with currants (spotted dick) my favorite and always will be. An extra-large dram of real old Scottish whiskey to complete the meal.

Penny showed me up to my room and as she parted she kissed me on the lips and whispered. "If you think it's a ghost coming into your room make no mistake it will be, but I will wait until mother is asleep for she is a heavy sleeper". True to her word Penny opened the door to my room and whispered "Move over Dexter and be ready to accept a passenger" She removed her nightdress and slipped in beside my naked body. It was for mutual satisfaction but no intercourse took place. I know she wanted to but with no condoms we would be taking a risk. Anyway, I would feel guilty if I had seduced her. That to me was sacred and only for Von unless I was drugged or drunk and incapable of refusal. At least when sober I did have self-control to a certain extent. If you might be curious if I told Penny I was married. I did indeed.

Twice I awoke during the night and felt Penny's body against mine and for a second I thought it was Von beside me. The second time I awoke Penny was not in my bed and as she said later Mother always rises early often by 5am. At 4 30 am she went back to her bed. Breakfast was out of this world, two eggs, a large portion of pudding, two slices of this bacon, two big flat pork sausages, an oatmeal cake, and two slices of toast. This was after a big plateful of hot porridge oats.

As I left their house to catch the train back to Inverness, I put my hand into my inside coat pocket and as I tried to withdraw it Penny restrained my hand from coming out. "You owe us nothing Dexter and we will be insulted if you offer us anything" she explained. I was forced to accept her hospitality without passing of any cash. Penny walked with me to the train station. "When you next in London you must come and stay at our house and meet my wife" I laughed and continued "but do not mention what we did on the train or in your mother's house." "Of course not, I promise on my life that your secret is safe with me Dexter, and thanks for making me happy" she smiled and then kissed me full on the lips with the taste of her tongue forcing its way into my mouth. I gave her my pager number and informer her "this is the best way to contact me as I am often out and about but will always hear the bleep on my pager and phone you wherever you are, however I must point out in two weeks' time I will be going abroad somewhere".

Chapter 14

AT LONG LAST I WAS OFF TO THE STATES

It had been a long time coming, 10 years to be precise. I had been to over 50 countries in Asia, Africa, Europe, Oceania, South and North America but never the States. I was assigned to be in the USA for 3 weeks covering news in Los Angeles. I would be brushing shoulders with some of the most famous actors in Hollywood. I flew from London airport and sat next to this guy who would not stop talking. He had been married 6 times and was going back to his native America to marry for the 7th time to his second wife. He gave me the book line and sinker on all his former relationships. His first romantic liaison was age 10 so he had me believe with a 14-year-old girl in the back of his father's car. He starred to tell me the sordid details but I stopped him I was in no mood to listen about sex with 2 under age kids. "Pleas Guy (as that was his name), I do not want to hear about forbidden love. In the UK, sex with minors is a criminal offence" Guy laughed. "Yes, well it is in the US too but we were both kids." Spare me the details Guy, "just tell me did you marry her?"

Nope, but we got it off again when she was 20 at her Father's ranch, and I can tell you that was real good." He explained stoking his chin. I put my hand up please Guy I don't wish to hear, it's your private life so keep it to yourself, I paused "No offence Guy, but I don't have the stomach for sexual relationships, I happen to be very happily married". He shut up for a little while but it was not long before he was telling me the reason he left his many wives. I was glad when the journey was over and we went our own separate ways. It was later I found out he was a well-known actor in Hollywood, but I did know him from Adam. His name was Chuck Lewis who featured in many westerns playing the bad guy.

No doubt you are wondering why my wife did not come with me. A simple reason really, an error in the issue of a visa. However, once that was sorted out she was to join me 4 days later. In the meantime, I was to link up with an old friend who it turned out was instrumental for me to be given an audience with Bob Hope, Frank Sinatra Jack Lemon and Tony Curtis, plus other less well known but on the way up.

I was sitting outside a café drooling over my second Budwesier, having just finished ta hot beef sandwich, when a friend from the past just happens to turn up. I found my eyes being covered by sweet smelling female's hands, and a voice that asked "Guess who this is Dexter?" I recognised the voice immediately, it was Penny, the lady on the train en route to Wick.

She sat down and we enjoyed a conversation that was most revealing. She had been married, but had not told me before when we first met. She had been in the States working on a film and fell in love with one of the actors, Lee Walsh. A whirlwind romance of just 5 weeks and they got married in Las Vegas.

PENNY'S STORY

"I was parted from Lee, my husband after about 3 weeks and had to go up to New York to appear in a B movie called *'something weird happen to me'*. The filming had finished a day earlier than scheduled and I flew back to LA and to the apartment we shared. I wanted to give him a surprise, so I unlocked the door quietly and crept slowly towards the bedroom. I paused when I could hear groans of ecstasy coming from the bedroom. I was expecting to find another woman in bed with my husband, but I got far more of a shock when she opened the door. He was sharing our bed but not with a woman, but a man whom I thought was just a good friend of my husband, not his homosexual lover. It was too much for me to take in so I stormed out of the apartment. I sued for divorce, and I am still waiting for the decree absolute".

"I made a few enquires about Lee and he friend and discovered that he had known his male love, Wayne long before he met me. He only married me for appearance sakes.

I left LA and came home and got work in the London in a couple of stage shows. That was 6 months ago. I never met anybody else until you and I met on the train to Wick. I took to you straight way, but don't get me wrong Dexter, I don't want to come between you and your wife, but sex with you was wonderful and would like a rematch if you are up for it, obviously no strings attached."

BACK TO MY STORY

Penny held my hand in hers, lifted it up to kiss it and also sucked my fingers. How could I resist her charms again? Momentarily I forgot that I was married to Von and like a lamb, I was led out of the café to her car arm in arm.

"My place or yours?" Penny asked. "Mine, I think as I am expecting a call at 11 pm from my agency" I suggested.

No sooner had we entered my apartment than Penny kicked off her shoes and piloted me towards the settee pressing her lips hard against mine at the same time discovering that I was hard. She wanted me badly and resisting would be futile. Her hands had already undone my belt and slid it out of the loops and laid it on the floor. Her hand inside my trousers and feeling my hardness on the outside of my Y fronts. It was not long before she stood up, swung my legs to the floor and removed my shoes before yanking down my trousers and y fronts to my ankles and then pulling them off and to bury her head between my legs.

A few minutes later before I had time to climax, she stood up and removed her dress to stand before me in her tights and suspenders. Slipping out of her knickers, I was able to see her bush which she was rubbing as she returned her mouth between my legs. "I want you to fuck me this time" she said as momentarily she lifted her head up to press her lips against mine. "Oh God Penny I don't have a condom". She stood up and walked over to her handbag and extracted a packet of three and commented with a smile "I do, so you get yourself into the bedroom and into bed and I will join you in just a minute. Like a good little boy, I obeyed and when totally devoid of all my clothes, I entered the bed. Penny now totally naked apart from her long hoop earrings slipped in beside me. Pulling my face to hers at the same time her lower body was pressed against my sex and I felt the tingling of her bush rubbing against my erection. Her hand methodically threads the condom on to my tackle and with no further foreplay, she mounted me and fed my sex into her sex. She was hardly silent as she pumped away until we both climaxed in unison.

So anxious was she for sex that we used all three condoms before morning. I took my phone call from Von and also from ONMA during out lovemaking sessions. To say Penny was sex hungry was an understatement, I would say sex starved. We would have more, had there been any more condoms. before breakfast and before I woke up she had slipped downstairs and acquired another pack of 3 and we did the deed again before she departed for the film sex. I dressed at the same time as she did and we parted with a long passionate kiss. The arrangements were that we would meet again that night, and promised she would try to obtain some meetings with a few select stars of Hollywood. She was true to her word, as I mentioned earlier.

Another night of unbridled passion and I wondered if I would have enough energy to satisfy Von when she arrived later that week. After our second night of passion, three more condoms filled I was introduced to the first of many stars who were all willing to give me an interview. I suppose Bob Hope was probably the one that will always remain in my mind. His comical turn of phrases and his warm attitude towards me will forever stay in my memory.

I never saw Penny again that week. It was just as well it would give me time to regain my strength for when Von arrived. I met her at the airport and she gave me our now expected long lingering kiss. She spoke about her flight seated next to a woman who was making her first flight and seemed very nervous. When they got into an air pocket and the aircraft shook somewhat she held onto my wife shaking like a leaf. However, the air turbulence did not last too long and the lady was able to relax, and free herself from my wife. She told me about the kids and what they had been up to. They sent me as always their love.

That night in my apartment we made love that lasted until way after midnight. I had no after effects of my liaison with Penny. Come morning, Von wanted to be satisfied again so I was playing the dutiful husband and obliged, we then showered together before I had to go to the studios for a few more interviews with the stars. Von decided to take this opportunity to take in the sights of LA with the wife of another journalist saying in the adjacent department. This other journalist was French as was his wife but both spoke good English. Von had spent some time learning a few languages, mostly the basics from me, sufficient to get by.

I concluded my interviews with a few more up and coming stars. By the end of the week, I had obtained nine interviews. The last interview completely out of the blue was with Ali Macgaw, I also met her husband Robert Evans. Ali had recently finished the film love story, which I had seen earlier in 1970. She was nominated for the academy award as best actress in that film. The directors of ONMA were very pleased with my efforts. In particular with Ali, Bob, Tony and Frank.

After a few more days in LA, I was instructed to go to New Orleans to cover the big musical festival being held there. Von and myself could not find anywhere to stay in the city, so we had to stay in a Laplace on lake Pontchartrain. It was a beautiful place and as we wanted to attend church being a Sunday, we found this little Baptist church not far from the hotel we were staying in. As we walked up the steps we were met by a white guy who looked at my wife and in an almost inappropriate manner exclaimed "No niggers in here boy, she can go to the black church the other side of town, but if she is your slave, you are welcome to enter our house of God, but not her." I was tempted to say something but in the end, my silence indicated my disgust at his unchristian attitude.

We went to the church on the other side of town. We were greeted by another man, a Negro who explained "We don't have many whites in this church, you are outnumbered 10 to

1 but if you want to come into our church, you are welcome". He paused "Is this lady with you who I see is of Filipino descent your wife". I nodded my head and he outstretched his hand and shook both our hands firmly. Then he pointed to the entrance to the church and bade us enter. The service was unlike I had experienced before a lot of singing and fire and brimstone rhetoric. We both admired the gospel singing and as we shook hands with the pastor as we left, he thanked us for gracing his church. We got into conversation with two other couples of mixed bloods. One was also from the Philippines and Von and who had since become more efficient in the language spoke with her. Both couples had to admit that from the white population there were a few racist perpetrators who disliked the black population. Albeit there was a strong Ku Klux clan element in the area. However, the black people in Laplace were well organized and the racist element did not dare to face confrontation.

In New Orleans the following day, I attended several of the music festivals with Von. We were very impressed with the soul singers and the dancing bands. Having recently been given tuition on the use of cameras. I found my ability to take some very good photographs to wire back to the agency. My opinion of my first visit to the Sates was mixed. In some instances, I found the negative side very upsetting in some white folk's opposition to the African American. However, I did not notice this negative side in LA and whites and blacks mixed freely. I was warned most strongly about activity in downtown LA that I should avoid as violence and drugs played a significant role in that part of town. Neither of us ventured there to either confirm or deny the stories, we had been told.

Chapter 15

LOVED BY TWO WOMEN

9th of August 1974 and President Nixon resigned as President of the USA following revelations on the Watergate scandal. Gerald Ford became the 38th President of the USA. I was there with Von three days before Ford became President and to cover his inauguration. We stayed in Washington for eight days afterwards covering the aftermath of his ascent to the highest office in the states. Von and I enjoyed the pomp and circumstances for her first visit to Washington DC with all the razzmatazz that followed.

Back home, my son Aqyza was getting ready for his first interview as a reporter with the Herts Herald. I stayed on in the States whilst Von returned home. My visit again to LA was not without I incident, as I had another reunion with Penny. It was totally out of the blue, and ironically it was the same café we had met in 1971. No hands round the eyes this time, she sat down in front of me inside the café. I looked up and my eyes almost fell from their sockets. "Hello stranger" she exclaimed. "So nice to see you again, you still married" She continued as she leaned over to kiss my lips. "Of course I am still married, in fact Von had just returned to England after she was with me for the inauguration of Gerald Ford" I responded. "So what about you married again, still working in Hollywood?" I enquired. "No, not married yet, did have an affair though that lasted 4 months with Joe Tucker the actor, but he was so moody and a bit violent at times so I had no part company with him, other than that just the odd dinner date with a few actors and film crew". She informed me. "So your sex life is a bit slow then" I suggested. Penny smiled. "Yes you could say that, no more one night stands, the last time I had sex with Joe was 8 months ago". She said nonchalantly, "What about you Dexter, your sex life as lively as ever." She continued. "Yes lively when I am with Von but no other extra marital affairs since with you here in LA in 1971 over three years ago" I informed her smiling as I did so. Penny put her hand on mine and whispered "You know Dexter sex with you was the best I have ever had and I am now spilt for choice" She paused and after clearing her throat and wiping a tear from her eye continued. "If only you were not married you would be my first choice, I never told you this before but after you went away to New Orleans, I never saw you again, I really missed you". Was the sock statement she made to me" "What are you trying to say Penny?" I ask enquiringly she breathed in deeply looked at me straight in the eye and announce in a positive tone "Dexter Barren I love you, and nothing will change that, but I understand we can never be together forever, but just to have you in my bed for a night would be heaven for me." I gripper her hand firmly "I don't know if it is possible to be attracted to another at the same time, but as soon as you sat down and I looked into your eyes and after that kiss we shared, I felt elated, excited something inside of me was happening and I can't explain. Maybe it is love that for you I have. Often over the last three years, I have thought of you. Seeing your body on the bed in LA and the time on the train in Scotland. You slipping into bed with me at your Mother's house in Wick. These thoughts will never leave my memory. The thought of you always causes a reaction in my lions". Penny gripped my hand even further and I felt her naked foot between my legs. Her toes rubbing against my crotch confirming that I was having a reaction, or should I say erection.

Within the hour we were in bed together sharing each

other's bodily affections. Complete abandonment as she sat astride of me and we enjoyed what we had not done for the past three years together. Not once but thrice before the morning sun awoke us from our slumber did we enjoy carnal gratification. It was in my apartment, not the same on as three years ago but just as nice. However, the surroundings were of no importance to us as it was the sex and loving devotion that was taking precedence for the sheer our joy of sharing each other's body.

I was only scheduled to stay in LA for a further eight days before returning to England and after a week's vacation, I would be seconded to the UN office of Information as a press officer. This would mean wherever UN peace forces were stationed I could be there as information and press officer.

Penny and myself met four more times whilst I was in LA for nights of passion and twice for a meal in good quality restaurants. If I was not in love with her before, I certainly was then. Parting from LA caused tears in both our eyes. I was going to miss her and she voiced the same. Somehow we would keep in contact. I gave her my PO box number c/o the united Nations Information office New York.

MY SON'S STORY

My mother was fussing over me before I left for my interview in St. Albans with the Editor of the Herts Herald. She wanted me to look my best and chose the right time for me in her opinion, whilst I wanted to wear the multi-coloured one my ex-girlfriend Michele had bought me for my 16th birthday in March. Michele and I had been an item for only months from February until April 1974. Although Dad met her once he neither said he approved or disapproved, but I sensed he was not considering her as my future wife. Michele and myself were always arguing and like my father I did not like arguments. My ex-girlfriend's parents always seemed to be arguing and her daughter though it was normal. I had never heard my parents argue or even raise their voices to each other. Perhaps it was because Dad was only home probably for about three months a year. The longest time he was ever away was a month and then when he was home.

Mum and my sister Linda had him with us for at least a week before he went away again.

I was envious of my father and from a very early age, I wanted to be news correspondent. I never wavered in this desire. Unlike my Dad, who never went to University for the right to become a journalist, in my time this wall all changed and for me to progress in my chosen career I would need a degree. I would spend two years on local newspapers, go to University and then present my credentials to National papers and News agencies. Dad encouraged me to learn Spanish, so I spent two summers whilst at school on an exchange visit with a Spanish student, Marcos. Dad always said that the two most important languages were English and Spanish. Mandarin if I want to, my grandmother taught me Tagalog the principle language of the Philippines where she was born. Both Dad, Linda my sister and I spoke it better than mum, although she had improved as we tried to speak it at home when grandmother was present, although she spoke perfect English it was felt that we should at least know that language in the event we might visit there in the future.

I was shown into the office of the Editor of the Herts, Herald. He put his hand out and shook it firmly observing my f ace before he commented "I can't help noticing how much like your father you look when he was your age, save to say your skin is darker, but that is natural giving your lovely mother is half Filipino" "So you met my father then?" I asked curiously. Of course Aqyza, I was a reporter on The Essex Rural Echo when he was there, and I was also at his wedding to your mother. Sadly, though we lost touch with each other when he joined the news agency in Australia. Recently though, I met him at a press conference in Liverpool and we had a drink to mull over the old days".

He informed me. Mr. Sidney Turner, the editor, asked me a few more questions about my education before shaking my hand and confirming I could have the job as a cub reporter. His final comment was "If you are half as good as your father, you will be a success".

When I got home and told mum and Linda the good news, the first thing Mum did was phone Dad in LA and I spoke to him too. He gave me some valuable advice that I took on board, as he had been a cub reporter with a local newspaper before I was born. Linda was looking forward to going to drama school as she had been in a few TV plays and her desire was to be an actress. Dad I remember saying in his younger days at school, he had taken to liking drama. However, when it came to choosing a career, he had a choice of being an actor, football player, journalist or grandfather's profession as a Chaplin. As we know he chose Journalism.

BACK TO MY STORY

I was so pleased that my old work friend Sid Turner had employed my son Aqyza. In y early days on the Echo, he had not only been a good friend but gave me valuable advice in the art of writing a good newsworthy story. I spoke to all three of my family before I returned to my sinful activity with Penny. I was in love with two women, but what could I do about it, I am only human. I was not even feeling guilty about my double life. If it were possible to have two wives, I would not have hesitated. Perhaps jokingly, I suggested to Penny "Perhaps I should change my religion to one that allows a man to have more than one wife" Penny smiled as she stretcher her hand out and pulled me back onto the bed. We were both naked as we rolled on the bed in mock wrestling that resulted in Penny becoming worst off as out fooling around resulted in her falling on the floor banging her head on the corner of a cupboard and loosing conscientiousness. I fell to my knees beside her and lifted her head. There was blood on her temple. I found a box of tissues on top of the cupboard and taking out two of them I bathed her head. There was a cut but thankfully it was not deep. I had done as much as I could, even to checking that she had a pulse. I lifted her motionless body onto the bed and laid a blanket over her. I sat for a few minutes cradling her head. I was wondering if I should call 911. She remained still as I walked over to the phone and began to dial 911 when a groan from the bed assured me that Penny was gaining consciousness. I put the phone back on the cradle and went back to the head. "What happened?" She enquired as she felt the lump on her temple. "You fell off the bed and hit the cupboard". I explained.

Penny soon recovered and after a glass of brandy was feeling one hundred percent better. She was very understanding that it was an accident and later cavorting on the bed again. I pushed the cupboard away from the bed just in case our further frolics resulted in one or the other or both falling on the floor. That was our last night together before I returned to England.

Chapter 16

SECONDED TO THE UN

Von, Aqyza, Linda and my mother all came to the airport to meet me. After kissing Von, Linda and my mother, I hugged my son "I congratulate you Aqyza on your job with the Herald, with Sidney Turner you won't have a better teacher, he taught me lots in my time at The Echo, and I think without his help I would not be where I am now" I finished hugging him and hand in hand with Von and Linda holding my other hand holding on to Aqyza, we went back to the car. Mother walked alongside at first holding Aqyza's hand until we came to a large pillar when she let go or would have collided with this obstacle.

It was nice to be home and in my own bed for a few days with my beloved wife and be with my children until my secondment to the UN. I had not expected to be going back to the USA so soon. I got the letter first then the phone call as a follow up to confirm that I was to be in New York on Monday the 9th of September. To the report to the head of the department Wayne Hudson (nickname Rock after the film star) at 9 am. I departed for New York on Sunday afternoon with Von driving me to the airport. I was only expected to be there for a week then be sent on assignment, but where I did not know. My flight to the USA was without incident and the flight I remember was on time. I needed time to recover from jet large as per normal with NY, 5 hours behind the UK.

I was introduced to Rock at just after 9am after I had met the eight other people who were to be on the training programme before we could go on assignment. Rock was a daunting figure in his late 50's of 6 feet 4 inches in height and towered over all the members on the induction course. We were formally introduced to each other before we underwent a course related to behavior on foreign soil where we would be ambassadors for the United Nations. There was a lot to learn so much that if I were to tell you all the rules and regulations we had to understand it would no doubt bore you to ears. I am trying to keep my promise I made at the start of this book that I would skip the boring parts.

All of us had been picked because we were linguists. Carol Bellman from Wales spoke the most languages, twelve in total. However, she did not speak Tagalog or Chinese but the 4 others more than me were Russian, Polish Lithuanian and of course her native tongue Welsh. As a group, we all got on very well despite none of us coming from the same countries. We all spoke at least three common languages Spanish, English and French. Carol from Wales, Sarah from Israel, Tania from Russia, Helgar from Germany, Mi Hoe from Hong Kong, Mohamed from Saudi Arabia, Kofi from Togo, Jacquest from France and myself. Five ladies, four men plus Rock. Total 10. At least there was no sex discrimination.

After the induction course that lasted for 4 days from 9 30 am to 4 30 pm with an hour for lunch each, we were ready to return to our own countries for a few days before going on our assignments. We all wished one another the best of Luck and I travelled back to the UK with Carol. She was not interested in men, as I had found out during the first day of the course as she was very close to Helgar, or tried to be until Helgar put her straight that she was straight. However, I could not say the same for Mi Hoe and for most of the course and evenings out, she and Mi Hoe were an item. The rest of us went out for a drink but there was no fraternization, although I often caught Tania smiling at Kofi as if they wanted to start something. The rest of us were just out to enjoy the beer.

Carol and myself sat side by side on the plane back to the UK. We talked a bit but only about our former assignments for our former employers. Carol last employer was the Daily Mail but had worked for other papers worldwide including 6 years in the US where she had worked for several state newspapers. She made no secret of her age 48 and though she had been married for 7 years obtained a divorce as she found her sexual preference was for her own gender, but did not rule out the odd fling with a man if he were older. That ruled me out at 34.1 said goodbye to Carol at Heathrow airport as she caught another flight to Cardiff. Von was alone when she met me at the airport and we went straight home. I was feeling tired after the trip so went to bed soon after a conversation with my children. Von joined me but alas was unable to perform my husbandly duties until the morning. Von was most understanding as she always was.

As we lay in bed that morning, she began to ask me about my job and how long would I continue to be working overseas. "You are 34 now and surely in the next year or two, you will give up and hopefully find gainful employment in the UK." She paused, kissed me on the cheek and continued. You know I do worry about you and every night I pray to God that he will bring you back safe to my arms and in my bed." I smiled, "Von you know I love this job and when you married me you were fully aware of what I wanted as a career and as much as I love coming home to you a few times a year, I can't see myself giving up just yet". I paused and yawned before I continued. I think our love is strong because I am not under your skin all the time so we don't have time to argue." Von smiled "You are right darling, I can't remember the last time we had a cross word" I have interjected "Last year, I was driving us home from the airport and I took the wrong turning and you said where you going this is the wrong way. I was feeling tired and shouted at you. I know what I am doing; you insisted I was going the wrong way. I told you to shut up. You told me to stop the car as you did not want to finish up going the wrong way. So, I stopped the car and you got out. I was about to drive off and leave you there when I came to my senses, I apologised to you. I saw the road sign and we were going the wrong way" Von smiled "I know about that, just wanted to see if you remembered" She leaned over to me and ran her fingers through my hair chest. "I could never stay mad at you for long" Her hand slid down the covers and rested between my legs then she swung herself over onto my lap and we made love making up for the week I was away.

I was issued with my blue Beret and this I was told to wear all the times along with my UN insignia on my arm. My deployment was to a country in East Africa where a recent uprising had existed. It was the job of the UN force to keep the peace between the former fighting factors. My job was to report on all incidents that occurred, however trivial. I had arrived in the early morning and was met by the camp commandant. He explained to me that the UN force was a mixture of African forces and European. He himself was

French. Over the next four hours I met most but no all the guys and girls of course. A mixture of languages but most they were French speaking. My little office was directly behind the Command HQ. And this was also the place, I would sleep. The terrain was mostly desert but a river nearby was in the wooden area.

It was there later that day a black soldier from West Africa showed me the river and we both swam there. As he stripped off, I noticed he had no modesty and the size of his middle leg made me feel inferior. I guess at the flaccid state it was a foot long and probably three in circumference. I shuddered to think what size it would be in its erect state. I followed him and stripped off totally myself before plunging into this water. "Hey Umbra, hope there is no crocodiles in this pond." No worry Mister Dexter, them crocs is nowhere near here you perfectly safe" I took his word and when we finally finished our bathing we sat on the bank. Just with my towel covering my lower regions. He still remained exposed. I tried no to look at his lower region although he was stroking it. I looked into his face "You married then Umbra" I asked. "I have 5 wives" he retorted "but now, I am out here I have no wife with me." Do you miss them?" I asked inquisitively. "Do you miss your wife?" was his response. "Yes, of course, but I only left her yesterday, and look forward to seeing her again in a month" was my answer to his question.

I could not help but notice that his appendage had indeed increased in size. I shuddered. "You ever held a black man's cock?" he asked as he stood up. I was ready to run after seeing it now fully extended at least protruding a good two-foot or more away from his crotch. "I am straight, very straight," I shouted out so get away from me with that thing. I had already started to dress and then picked up the rest of my clothes and started to walk back to the camp and run if necessary. "Don't worry Mister Dexter I is not going to touch you I'm getting ready for the two girls you see over yonder" He indicated two slim black girls without their tops on and displaying their ample proportions standing beside the trees only a few yards away. I realized that this was his entertainment. I took my leave of him and from the corner of my eye I saw both girls approach him having removed their lower clothing. I had never been a voyageur, but on this occasion I was curious to see what he would do. I hid behind a tree, but close enough to see both girls handling his massive weapon with their hands and mouths. I must admit watching this activity did arouse me a little. I could not imagine that he would penetrate either of these young women. To take his entire massive weapon inside their vagina would surely have done an injury to them. I had seen enough.

I returned to my cabin adjacent to my office. Relevant or not I did record this incident, but not the name of the soldier. I was feeling tired so I lay down on the bed careful to make certain my mosquito net was fixed properly. I must have been dozing for a short while when my sleep was disturbed by a door being opened. Standing in the doorway I could make out a native girl who later I was to find out was just turned twenty. She had short curly tight hair and very slim, bare feet no more than five feet high. At first I thought it was a young boy. She was dressed in a white dress that covered her body to below the knees. I lifted up my body up in the bed holding the blanket CO cover my nudity and asked. "Who are you" as there was no reply, I repeated the question in French, *(qui vous etes)* She replied (*Je suis votre fille maison queje vinss de nettoyer votre cabine et de faire vos enchires que vous avez besoin, Mon nom est Malibu*") "I am your house girl I come to clean your cabin and do your bidding as you require, my name is Malibu" She explained. I pulled the blanket, round me and got up from the bed." I suggested, "Come back tomorrow unless you have anything urgentyou need to do. (*"Je nettoie et la poussiere est maintenant que you OK"*) I clean and dust now is that OK" she requested. I let her carry out these chores but did not sleep again until she had finished.

I woke in the morning early and after dressing in khaki shorts, white shirt, blue beret and the UN insignia armband I took my self-off to the bulge in the river. I surveyed the area first for unwanted animals or other human beings. None of the afore mentioned present I undressed and slid my naked body into the coolness of the water. I had not been there long as I clung to the side of the bank out of sight of anybody who would pass bye on either side of the river. The two black girls I had seen yesterday with Umbra were on the opposite side of the river. I watched them disrobe each other from their scanty clothing and enter the water hand in hand. I stood and watched as they began to wash each other. I had known about lesbians for some time but until that time I had not seen them in any carnal activity. I watched as they kissed each other in the water and their hands massaging each other's bodies above and below the water. I kept silent as in awe I watched their performance. After about a few minutes of their embracing and carnal activity they swam for a further period before leaving the water dressing and walking away hand in hand pausing a few times to kiss each other on the lips.

I returned to my cabin and Malibu was dusting the furniture. She enquired if I had any clothing to be washed. I shook my head. *(Lorsque vous avez, vient de mettre dans le panier et je vais le faire pour vous)* "when you have, just put it in the basket and I will do it for you" she continued. I made certain that my private things were secure in a locked draw before I went to my office next door.

I had a number of documents that I had to read and sign and do a brief report from information supplied. I had to translate from the French and put it into understandable English. Once this was done I used the telex to send it to UN HQ in NY.

By the time I had returned to my cabin, Malibu had finished cleaning my cabin and she had also tied up my clothes and made my bed. She was lying on the floor sleeping by the window. I did not want her to be disturbed so I tip toed past her. I decided to make myself a cup of tea and then I sat on the chair and observed her sleeping. She reminded me of my house girl in Ghana. She was the same build small and compact and barefoot but she was much darker than Precious. Watching her face, she seemed to have a smile on her face, probably having a nice dream. She was laying on her back her legs slightly apart and her scanty dress had ridden up above her knees exposing part of her bottom, her head resting on a cushion she had taken off the sofa. I gently leaned over and laid a blanket over her body, as I thought she was not aware that she was showing so much skin. She must have been half awake as she pulled the blanket off her body, as she did more skin was exposed as her dress had rode up again even further to expose that she wore no underwear. Was this her intention to tease me? I decided that I would not succumb to temptation as I stood up and walked into my bedroom where I lay on my bed. I had been warned on many occasions that black girls particularly in some regions of Africa did have sexual fantasies towards white men.

I woke up to the sound of running water in the washing room. I decided to investigate. The door was wide open and Malibu was naked in front of the sink and using a cloth was washing her body. Curiosity would not let me divert my eyes. She looked up and saw me but made no attempt to stop what she was doing, just the opposite she turned to face me, it was then that I was see that she had a petite breast. She started to wash between her legs. This was a clear indication that she wanted me to watch her. I was memorised. I suggested to her that she could use the shower. She ignored this suggestion and just carried on doing the same as before. I was not going to give in to temptation. The signals she was giving me were no doubt providing an invitation for me to take advantage. I was not going to be the one that made the first move in case this was not a deliberate act to entice me or just the natural way for her to behave.

I moved away from the doorway and went back to the bed. Trying to control my animal instincts. I was feeling hot and needed to take a shower. Shortly after I heard her leave the washing room was my cue to go and use the shower myself. The water was cold as there was no means of heating it, not that one needed hot water in this climate. I do not know where Malibu was, it seemed as if she had left the cabin and I was in a safe position to shower without being disturbed. To operate the shower, I had to pull on a lever to pump the water up through the system. The water cascading on to my body was cooling me. I realized that the soap was still by the sink. I stepped out of the shower to fetch it just as Malibu walked back into the washing room. She was still naked and seeing I was the same moved towards me and touched my chest with her hand running her fingers down to my navel, pausing before grasping my sex in her hand. I was not in control of my emotions and let her have what she wanted. She held onto me. Her face was now resting on toy chest and her arms encasing my body. There were no words spoken. Her lips pouted for me to kiss her. This I did. She led me into my bedroom and lay on the bed and patted the space beside her an indication for me to lay or sit there. I did as she suggested and she laid her head on my chest. All this was done in silence.

I must have drifted off to sleep for when I awoke Malibu had gone and darkness had descended. I quickly realized that before she had left she had arranged the mosquito net round the bed. I got up and took a beer out of the bucket. Not quite cold but sufficient for it to quench my thirst. Returning to bed I laid there and tried to recollect the actions that had gone before. I was aware only that we had laid together, also very certain that I had not seduced her.

Over the remainder of my stay in this part of Africa Malibu was content just for me to hug her, either naked together or clothed. She had lost both her parents in the civil war and the man she was due to marry. She was 20 but looked older than her age. She wanted to be loved as with the loss of her folks her life had been severely damaged. She enjoyed assisting me under the shower and I reciprocated. I never tried to seduce her and I don't think she wanted me to either. She was in her element just to lie on the bed with me encompassed in my arms and head on my chest and assist me under the shower. I did not know if she was giving the same service to the other soldiers on the campsite, but it was not my concern, she was a free agent. If she was to be believed she told me no other man was touching her since her boyfriend had been killed some 3 months earlier on the same day as her parents and two brothers.

Letters from Von and Penny were delivered to me every

week. I had to be careful where I kept the communications from Penny. I did not want Von to find them. I had created a secret lining in one of my bags where I could secret them until I was able to put them in my strong box in my bank in Borehamwood. I always read Von's letter first and the attachments by Aqyza, Linda and my mother. Last but not least I read Penny's letter. Always asking when I would next be in the States or the UK. Of course I was unable to give a precise date for the USA, although gave her the dates I would be on leave in the UK. The week before I was due to return home the last letter from Penny told me she would be in London and looking forward to meeting me again. She suggested a time and date at Paddington station. In my letter to her I confirmed I would be there.

There were no more incidents worthy of my writing about in the last few weeks before I left Africa. There were tears in Malibu's eyes as I bade her farewell. I told her that I would be returning after my vacation in London. This seemed to make her less depressed at my parting. An African lady called Isabel Gallerias who I had met before when I was in Ghana filled my place during my two-week vacation. I shook her hands and brought her up to date on the information I had compiled and forwarded to NY. This was essential so she would not duplicate what I had already dispatched to UN HQ.

Chapter 17

I CAN'T PULL OUT

Von met me at the airport and she drove home in partial silence until we were clear of the airport. I told her as much as I could about my stay in Africa obviously leaving out the carnal episodes. At home, Aqyza now given the nickname at work, son of News hawk or News hawk mark 2. Linda was in rehearsal for a film being shot at Elstree studios, and was to inform me that she had been accepted at drama school in London.

I went to meet Penny at Paddington Station. I was there early. The time arranged to meet was past and I realized that the letter she might not have received in time. I started to walk into the station in case she was waiting other than the place I had suggested. I heard her voice "Dexter I am here, I got delayed on the tube it broke down in the tunnel". She was right behind me. We faced each other and enjoyed a long lingering kiss. We had not seen each other for over a month. "What excuse did you give to your wife for you being away overnight?" she asked as our lips parted. "I told her I was seeing an old friend, which is not exactly lie". Was my response. Penny tucked her arm into mine and we headed for the platform that would take us to Reading.

The guesthouse was on the outskirts of the town. Pre booked the day before we met. It was early evening when we arrived so after unpacking our bags we took ourselves off to a restaurant for a meal. I had a couple of beers whilst Penny enjoyed two glasses of red wine. We walked around for about ten minutes looking in the shop windows and catching up on our recent past news. She laughed when I told her about the black guy and his very large appendage. I did not mention my sexual activity with Malibu only to say that she worked for me.

Once we were in the bedroom of the guesthouse, we both undressed separately. She in the bathroom and myself in the bedroom. I was naked standing before her whilst she was in a long white silk nightdress "You taking that off?" I asked. Penny smiled "no you can" she ordered. I did lifting her garment off over her head and once more feasting my eyes on her delights. My face buried her breasts as her hands were grasping, my bottom pulling me gently towards her. I paused our clinch as I went over to my coat and took out the packet of condoms. She took them from me and threw them the floor and exclaimed "You don't need these we can do bare back" "What if I can't pull out in time?" I exclaimed. She kissed me full on the lips and replied "I am on the ill so no need to pull out this time, I want to feel your climax for real, not caught in some piece of rubber."

That night I was to enjoy love making twice. I did not want to exhaust myself, as I knew Von would want me when I got home in the evening. I did not want her to have any suspicion of my infidelity. In the morning, we took a shower together and teased each other before taking breakfast paying the bill and returning to London. Penny was staying with friends in London for another night before flying up to Inverness and then the train to Wick. She told me that she was only staying in Scotland for a week before she returned to London to be in a film at Elstree Studios and would be there for about 6 weeks. My heart leapt, Penny was in the same film as my daughter Linda. I briefed Penny about my daughter and asked her to introduce herself, with the hope, I was not playing with fire'.

Von and myself went up to Hempstead to see my brother Dean, wife Sally and the kids. We stayed for four days and Dean showed us round the farm. It seemed every time we visited the farm he had acquired more acres, and new buildings were replacing those that my Grandfather had built before the last war. Many of the older building where the pigs lived and the stables were located were relics of the either the 18th or 19th century going back to my great great grandfathers' time. Might even be further back as the farm had been in my family since 1642. I hardly recognised the farm from my youth. The house had been modernised and the overall width and length was incorporated into the final structure from the original 9 rooms to 10 with the all four bedrooms doubled in size, plus an additional room as his study come farm office and a large conservatory. This new look mansion hardly recognisable from the house my grandfather lived in. Expanding the kitchen to double the original size. Doubled the size of the lounge and built an extra bathroom en suite. The old cobbled lane was now transformed into a tarmac road, still remaining a single-track road, but with two passing places in the half-mile length. In my grandfather's day the poultry were free range. In 1974, they had all been housed in heated hen houses. Dean had certainly established his talent and entrepreneur expertise on Morris Farm with the estate under his umbrella now being almost treble the size since grandfather died.
We left the farm on Monday morning with a selection of quality meat that had been reared and slaughtered in his own slaughterhouse. Free range eggs of which he kept twenty birds in the back garden for home and family use. Also from Sally's garden a selection home grown produce. I almost forgot to mention the garden had been expanded too. It took us just under two hours to get back to Elstree, given the roads were not used to handling so much traffic. Improvements were being made but were unable to handle the increase of vehicles that had more than double quadrupled since I was a youth.

Linda came home all excited and exclaimed "Daddy, guess who I met today at the film studios?" "Tell me Linda, who did you meet?" I asked knowing myself who it was. Linda sat down in the armchair and kicked off her flat shoes. And began "This Lady Penny Wise came up to me and asked my name, when I told her it was Linda Barren, she asked me if I was related to Dexter Barren the, international correspondent with the UN. When I said yes, she told me that she knew you and had met you in LA in the states and she was the person that got you all those interviews with Tony Curtis, Bob Hope, All McGraw etc." Von was privacy to this conversation as she stood by the kitchen door and interrupted "I thought you said it was Benny Wise" "No darling I clearly said Penny, you must have miss heard me," I suggested. then I chuckled "You are not getting jealous that I know this famous actress are you " Von smiled "No but I would love to meet her, she certainly did you a favour in LA getting you to meet all those stars Linda stood up and took a biscuit off the plate on the table and looking at me exclaimed "Guess what, she asked me if you were still abroad, when I said you were back in the UK and would be home this evening, I invited to come and meet you again, I hope I did not do wrong" She looked at Von for the expected reply "No Linda it would be nice to meet her", she paused "She is coming is she".. "At first she refused but I persuaded her to come by telling her that you make wonderful cakes, she said I love homemade cookies and agreed to come at about 8 pm". Linda explained.

At just after 8pm a taxi pulled up outside her house and a lady got out in a black wig and glasses. It did not look like Penny. I did know that when she was on set she wore a black wig so that when she was in public people would not recognise her. Also when in public she used the name Penny Hart instead of Penny Wise her theatrical name. Von opened the door to her and welcomed her to sit down. My acting skills came to the fore as I pretended that I had not seen her since LA almost two months ago. Once in the sanctuary of our home she removed her wig and both Linda,

Aqyza and Von looked shocked. "You look totally different without a wig on" exclaimed Linda. I took our dog Hover out *(so called because she would eat anything from the floor including all the crumbs)*. The rest of the family were happy to converse with Penny. I trusted her explicitly not to reveal too much about our relationship.

It was past 10 pm and Penny was kept busy talking about her film career. Linda was to play her daughter in the film <u>*Do not tell the kids*</u> being shot at Elstree studios and was talking about her role in the film. As I walked in Penny smiled "I suppose I better be going or I will miss the last train back to London. Totally out of the blue Von suggested that if she wanted to she could spend the night in our spare room. Penny did not take much persuading. Von and Linda made up the spare bed. We carried on talking with Penny until 11pm. I was being very careful by not showing any emotions towards Penny at the same time trying not to exasperate the situation by being too amorous with Von, although as Penny had said to me many times she did not want to break up my family and felt no jealousy toward Von. Many times she told me "Dexter if I can share you with Von or anybody else for just a few short meetings, I don't want any other man long term" .

Penny explained that she was not required on set until the afternoon and suggested that to avoid any inconvenience. She would leave the house when the rest of the family do. Von interrupted her "Aqyza leaves for work at 8 am and I drop Linda off at her school at 8 30 before I go to the charity shop to work for the morning" She paused and asked "what time do you have to be in studio?" Penny smiled "not until the afternoon when Linda has to be there too" Von grimaced "look you don't have to go when we go, my husband will be here so stay until you have to go, and I am sure he will make you breakfast or whatever, it's the least we can do. Penny chuckled "Do you trust me alone in this house with your husband?" Von laughed "Dexter spends almost 9 months away from me every year. All I pray for is he comes back to me in one piece still loves me and has not contracted any nasty diseases that is all any wife in my position can hope for.

Von and I made love that night and in the morning she got up dressed first and made breakfast for all the family. When she looked in on Penny she was still asleep, and did not disturb her. I dressed casually and sat at the table to eat with the family. Aqyza had left soon after finishing his cereal, and a half hour later I kissed Linda and Von goodbye, I read the local newspaper and tuned into the news on the TV. There was no movement from Penny in the spare room so I decided to check to see if she was ok. As I put my hand on the door- knob. I could hear her moving about in the room, so I knocked loudly twice. "Is that you Dexter?" she called out, and promptly open the door. She was wearing a nightdress loaned to her by Von. Given Von's stature at five foot and Penny at nine inches taller the nightdress barely covered her lower torso. She threw her arms round me and whispered "How long have we got before your family returns?" "Long enough" I replied as I steered Penny towards the bed and lifted off the only fabric that covered her enchanting charms. Devoid of my clothing curtsey of the skillful hands of Penny we both slipped in-between the sheets. I had enough passion and strength to take her, as she wanted bare back and deep inside. We enjoyed an hour of passion before we went downstairs dressed and I made her some breakfast.

Von was the first to return home from her voluntary work in one of the local charity shops. Although a qualified solicitor, she was having a break from the law to concentrate on bringing up the family. She told me that she would go back into the law once Linda had left school. It was her decision at least having a part time job she was not chained to the kitchen sink 24 7. Penny was ready to go to the studio and suggested that she wait for Linda and they could share a cab.

Chapter 18

HE FELL INSTANTLY TO HIS DEATH

It was time for me to leave for the airport and return to my post in Africa. Von drove me to the airport and saw me off for my second month on loan to the UN. It was an uneventful flight. However, driving on the unmade roads back to the UN camp was certainly not comfortable as we bounced around on the track. Our African driver did not consider our comfort, as he sped along eager to deliver his passengers to their destination. My two companions were both French soldiers one black the other white. Both men were returning from leave.

As I carried my bag into my cabin, I was met by Isobel with whom I shared two cups of tea whilst she brought me up to date on the recent activities. As we talked, I noticed the bruising on her face and asked her how she got it. Apparently, one of the white soldiers got him self-well intoxicated and tried to take advantage of her. She was not sparing in inhibitions as she relayed the story to me. As she was not very fluent in English, I have translated her story into English.

ISORELS STORY

"I was walking back from the canteen and very disappointed at the poor quality of food I was served with. I was only a few yards from the cabin. I felt my arms, being grabbed and he my assailant a white soldier pushed me to the ground. He was much bigger than I was and stronger too. I tried to push him off but he held me down and had my shirt undone and his hands were mauling my chest. His other hand was across my mouth then he was trying to pull my shorts down but I managed to keep my legs firmly closed. I remember he slapped my face several times. I could not scream as his hand on my mouth made this impossible to do. If it had not been for the other white soldier pulling my assailant off, I shudder to think what would have been the outcome. This other soldier my rescuer had hit my attacker with the butt of his rifle in the back of the neck. It was a fatal blow and we had to inform the camp commandant. He was very undemanding and conducted the investigation himself. No blame to my rescuer as he had acted in my defence"

BACK TO MY STORY

I bade farewell to Isobel and told her to enjoy her leave and looked forward to seeing her in 4 weeks' time. I went to kiss her on the cheek but she held my head and kissed me on the lips. I went to pull back but she wanted to enjoy the kiss more. I did not fight her willingness to taste my mouth. When she was finish, she smiled and said in broken English "Dexter you supreme kissing man". Isobel was only five foot in height and a little on the large size particularly in the bosom department. I think she could have suffocated me those massive breasts.

Why is it that all the black females I have met have design on me, come to that many of the non-white cultures too? I should try and control my emotions but how can one resist being kissed by any woman, so long as they are not in the ugly league. That reminds me of several new-year parties I was attending in other parts of the world. I had sore lips from being what I can best describe as over kissing. Some of the ladies went too far forcing their tongues between my lips. Some of them were the worst for drink and I could taste many varieties of alcohol on their tongues. I remember one year when I was in Belgium and one of the girls that kissed me or was it two had bitten into my lip. It took a few days to heal so I was sporting a big lump on my lower lip. Kissing was off limits. Just as well it had healed up before, I went home on leave to Von and the family.

I did not see Malibu until the following day. It was just after 6 am when she walked into my bedroom pulled aside the mosquito net and laid a kiss on my lips to wake me up. She slipped her naked body in beside me and just wanted to lay her head on my chest and play with my torso hairs. We lay together for about 15 minutes when I got out of the bed and informed her I was going for a swim. She pulled on her white dress and followed me to the bulge in the river. We both swam naked and she was playful throwing water over my face and grasping my appendage under the water. I lifted her up several times and tossed her into the water, she liked this and she was full of laughter. I then brought her attention to a couple of spectators, two natives both male watching us. She shouted at them in her local dialect and they moved away.

Back in the cabin, I had plenty of reports to make out and Malibu carried on with her chores. When she finished she hugged me round the waist kissed me gently on the lips and proceeded to her other duties around the camp. I had only just completed my report and ready to telex the UN office in NY when I heard gunshots. I froze because there was more than one shot and in rapid succession, convincing me it was an automatic weapon. I retrieved my pistol from the box under my bed and moved towards the window keeping out of sight. A black soldier from one of the rebel groups was firing wildly. A number of bodies lay on the ground wounded or dead. He was backing away from the scene of carnage cowards my cabin. With his back to me, I had one chance to stop his further massacre. I had no alternative but to shoot him in the back of the head for instant death. I went to the cabin entrance and hiding behind the door, I fired two shots in rapid succession. They reached the target and he fell instantly to his death.

The commandant congratulated me on my quick thinking. However, my action was too late to save the lives of the four soldiers who had been killed and three who were wounded. None of the soldiers though armed were unable to fire their weapons. This action had all taken place in a matter of just one minute. I remembered looking at my watch when I heard the rapid fire and after I had killed the sniper. It was five past 10 and when I looked and after I had fired my shots it was 6 minutes past.

A full enquiry was held into the shooting at the camp. We were all told to be more careful and the guards on the main gate were increased. For the next few days, I was in fear of my life in case another renegade was to try and get into the camp or in the close proximity. So it was that I did not go swimming again in the bulge for at least 6 days and when I did go I was accompanied by two soldiers and swam alone and never with Malibu again.

Malibu was taken away from the camp by some relatives and I never saw her again. In front of her uncle and aunt she shook my hand. And went with them to her new home, I was told by the commandant that she had wondered up to the camp gates pleading for work. It just happened that the one of the girls who had worked in the camp before Malibu asked for a job had been taken ill with malaria and had been flown out by the mission air service to a hospital in the capital. The commandant interviewed and was happy that she was a suitable replacement. It was only later after she had gone that I knew her real age 16. I was shocked as I was under the impression she was 20. At least I had not impregnated her. I would never forgive myself if I had fathered an illegitimate child in and African state where life was not appreciated by the military rebel factors, and rape was a prominent peril. When I went into the nearby village with armed bodyguards, I saw for myself that many women had been raped and given birth to offspring. There were white kids that looked out of place indicating to me that white mercenaries fighting with the rebels had used some of the women for their sexual satisfaction. I could never rape anybody it's not in my character. I have a hatred for the act of rape and feel these people that do it must be sadistic in their nature. When I have sex, I like to feel that whoever my partner is they are enjoying it as much as I am. Without the partner enjoying the act of love making it's not enjoyable. If Von refused to let me make love to her, it would be for a good reason, and I would respect it. Not even try to attempt to do anything against her will. The same went for other ladies who I met. It was normally the lady that made the chase and was the hunter. I am the pursued.

My replacement house girl was in fact not a girl but a boy not very efficient but as I had to tell him several times what he had to do. After a week, Isobel relieved me at the end of my second 4-week period. We shared a pot of tea together and I told her about the action in relation to the intruder.

She listened intently, then told me with a chuckle she already knew about the incident but that hearing it from me was as she said using a translation from the English into French "Out of the horse's mouth". I was due to leave on the same transport that had brought Isobel to the camp. However, there was a mechanical problem with this vehicle and as darkness had ascended before it was repaired. I had to stay another night. Can you guess? Of course you can I had to spend the night in the same cabin. I slept on in the chair despite Isobel asking me to share the bed. She was tempting me as I saw her totally disrobe and turn her body in my direction and whispered *("Suis-je vous faire suscite Dexter, mon offre est toujours ouvert")* roughly translated means. "If I attract you Dexter the offer is still open" I was tired and I knew that in the morning at first light I would be driven back to the airport along the rough track that was a poor substitute for a highway. I declined yet again, but she was persistent and walked towards me gyrating her body in such a way that I almost gave in at that precise moment and the kiss full on my lips with her holding my head. I had to admit the taste of her lips was delicious. My refusal was upsetting her but I was strong and self-control kicked in. She walked to the bed and got between the sheets. It was not the first time I had refused a lady's advances and probably not the last given my handicap of being a magnet to women. It can be a disaster this ability as more than once it has attracted the wrong women. Reminding me Hell hath no fury like a woman scorned.

I found it difficult to skep in the chair and I very much wanted the bed, but Isobel was in it. She could see I was having trouble sleeping and altered her request somewhat to imply I could sleep on the bed but not under her sheets. I kept my clothes on that night and slept on the same bed. I respected the fact that she never enticed me further. There would not be any consensual sex. Thankfully when we parted in the morning there was no recriminations. I did accept one of her sloppy kisses and the hand on my baby maker I did not remove straight away.

At last I was free of her and on my sexy to the airport. The journey I wanted but never enjoyed as the soreness of my body at the end of the trip to the airport had to be tolerated for a few hours on the plane. At least the plane took off on time and with few passengers on the flight I had nobody sitting next to me that would attempt to plague me with boring tales. The only aggravation was from a rather over active kid who had to be restrained several times from running up the aisle.

Chapter 19

I TOLD HER I KILLED A MAN

Von met me at the airport and our usual long lingering kiss. She drove home and the sound of music and the hustle and bustle of everyday traffic made me realize I was back to civilisation. I had six more tours in that camp in Africa, I can't say after all that happened I was looking forward to it again after my leave two weeks leave, I was silent on the journey taking in my thoughts, Von asked me "Is anything wrong Dexter? you have hardly said a word since we left the airport" I looked at her with a sedate smile and responded. "I'm thinking about what happened in Africa" Von pulled off the road as we came up to a long lay bye, and after parking switched off the engine and held my hand. "If something is a worry to you tell me, and don't tell me it's nothing. I got to know you and your mannerisms for over 19 years, and I know something is not right so tell me as we don't move from here until you do". She demanded sternly. I knew that I had to tell her, I had not put the shooting incident in any of my knees and now as she sat with me she was aware that something was a worry to me. She took my right hand and clasped her hands over it. Gently shaking it. I took a deep breath and began "I had to kill a man" Von's mouth open wide and enquired "why and how?"

By the time we pulled away from the lay bye I had told her everything in relation to the killing. She was physically upset but there was no way I could hide the sheer horror of the first time I had killed a man. If I had my way I would have told her many years on, not so soon after the incident. We both let tan run down our cheeks as the shock of what I had done was making itself evident now. What the medical people called delayed shock. By the time we reached home, I was feeling a little better, but I realized that Von was feeling rough. She was sharing my guilt at killing a nun, but I had no choice if the intruder had seen me I would have been another of his victims.

I tried to hide my feelings of depression that I was feeling after sharing my horrendous story with Von. Thankfully neither Linda at first and Agra and later when her got home noticed my torment, I was too elated at the news Linda gave me that Penny had persuaded the producer of another film to use her in his new film. It was to be located in the States. Here she was going to the USA at age 15 and I had to wait until I was 30 before I was to go these. I shared her excitement and I agreed she could go always providing that

Penny would take care of her. Von also agreed and when Penny came to the house we gave bee our decision.

Whilst I was away, Penny had been invited to stay in our house and accepted. As she put it. "It is better than staying in a hotel in London where the only people there chat I know are in the film business, boring film crewmembers, and a particular old fart that keeps pestering me to go out on a date with him". Linda and Penny had become very close in the month I was away and her extra tuition in the field of drama for Linda had been an asset to her education. The fact that Penny was my mistress convinced me that she would be ideal to protect Linda from whatever, or whoever.

It was my son who had been appointed to the Elstree Studios as the journalist to interview the stars of the three films being shot there. Top interview was with Penny Wise re Hart. My son and daughter had taken to Penny as an Aunt, and Von as her sister that she never had. Penny was now part of my fatally though neither ray children nor Von realized that she was my mistress.

It was later that evening that I took our dog Hoover out for his constitution. I went to the park and let her off for a run as I went behind the cricket pavilion and waited for Penny. Ten minutes later Penny arrived and we embraced for a sweet kiss. It was not for long. as Hoover wanted to play. I briefly had the chance to explain to Penny that I was a murderer and the full explanation of the shooting. She felt sorry for me and consoled me as I was still suffering from delayed shock. She then went onto explain that she was going to Wick tomorrow to stay with her mother and then back to the States. She hoped that Linda would join her on the flight in a week's time. as filming on the new production *'Sadly I am a Fool'* would commence. An application for a visa had been applied for and all that remained now was for her to be ready to leave in a week.

I drove Penny to the Radlett station and took a diversion, so we could have one last kiss and fumble before she got on her train to begin her long journey to Wick. I watched the train pull out of the station heading North. She realized that she would have to change at Bedford and again at Glasgow and Inverness so the last part of her journey to the North West coast of Scotland. I drove back into the town after parking my car I went to the Charity shop where Von worked. I had offered my service of a couple of hours as the manageress of the shop had a dental appointment. Von would be that alone. It was not that she could not cope on her own but it was always better to have somebody else to assist if she got busy.

It was just as well that I was there as we had a little bit of excitement. A young man was acting in a rather strange fashion, before I got to the shop. Apparently he had walked past several times and looked into the shop, Von was alone. Once I got there she informed me of this character and I believed he was up to no good. I decided to test my theory that he was planning to rob the shop. We both went into the back of shop and I was observing the counter from a spy hole in the wall. I was right. The charity shop was an easy target as the till was in full view of the street. As I suspected he ran into the shop and forced the till open, at the same time he had not expected a man to forestall him. He had a wad of notes already in his hand and picked up an ornament and threw it at me. It missed me. I lunged at him and with rugby tackle brought him down on the deck.

So my rugby experience did come in handy. though I did despite that sport.

Von called the police as I held onto the robber and to their credit they were there within a few minutes. He was led him away by two officers and a third officer asked Von and myself to make a statement. This was not apparently his first shop robbery, and in the last few weeks so we were informed he had helped himself to money from at least 6 other shops in Borehamdwood and Radlett I rang my son at the Herald and gave him the full story.

Penny stayed at our house overnight, but I had no opportunity to cavort with her. Linda was so excited at the prospect of going to the States she hardly slept at all that night. It was an early flight and Penny said Linda had to be at the airport by 6 am. An hour's drive at that tune of the morning. The whole family got up and had an early breakfast. I drove Linda and Penny to the airport, although Von wanted to come but she was so tearful at home having to say goodbye to our daughter, that it would be doubly worse if she displayed emotions in a public place.

My only kiss from Penny was hurried as Linda went into the toilets. at the bathroom. I had a tear in my eye for both

Penny and Linda. For my daughter it was to be a very big step in her life in the Media entertainment industry. I drove home after I had seen them enter into the departure lounge I kissed them both on the check as they took their leave of me.

I was back in Borehamwood at just after 7 am. My son was already up and Von was just coming down the stairs to make his breakfast. I drove him to the station and when I got back Von was reading the newspaper. We had not indulged in love making that night, as with an early start we both needed our sleep. I put my arms round my wife and kissed her neck. She brought her hands onto the top of my head and ruffled my hair. I then moved round to be in front of her. She was still in her dressing gown and a light nightdress underneath. I opened her robe via the cord around her waist pulled it open and felt the firm mounds of her upper body as our lips were melted together. She led me upstairs to our bedroom and as we both removed our clothing we fell onto the ben and with the radio playing sweet music we indulged ourselves in foreplay before penetration was the culmination of our love.

I was expecting to go back to Africa but owing to the circumstances of the shooting my employers the UN thought it better than my next posting should not be in that camp. The alternative they offered me was on the Pakistani Indian boarder. I knew it was a strife torn area, but I would be in a very secure camp on the Indian side of the border. Von as usual was a little worried at my new posting but realized this was my job. She would only have our son at home with Linda due to be in the USA from six to eight weeks.

My last night at home with Von and as we went to bed early we spent over and hour talking. Her concern was when I would stop being on international duties and perhaps work for a national paper in the UK. I was perhaps selfish in my desire to still be willing to travel to anywhere in the world. Von never asked me to surrender my international travel status, just wanted to know for the future when I would put it aside in favour of staying in the UK.

Von drove me to the airport that afternoon and 1 boarded the plane to New Delhi devoid of incident. I sat next to an Indian girl who was going to meet her fiancé for the first time. She was only 19 slim and dressed in a traditional sari. It was arranged marriage by her parents". I enquired "are your parents not travelling with you" She wiped a tear from her eyes! and after accepting my handkerchief to stem further tears she continued. "My parents were killed in a road accident in Yorkshire three months ago and my brother is in is in a comma in Leeds infirmary" "Why did you not stay in Leeds with your brother?" I enquired. She rubber her hands together before continuation. "I made a promise to my Father as he lay in the hospital bed and he told me to marry Jamul, as he was to badly hurt he said he would not survive the night. I told him not to be a pessimist as a modern medicine and surgery would save him. He held my hand and said Usher my life is over, I am being called to my new life, you will not see any life in my body after this night has past. I stayed with him holding his hand and shortly after his last words to me life went out of his body, and joined my mother who died instantly in the car accident". "What about your brother then who will take care for him?" I enterrupted. His wife is by his side and I know he is in good hands, but I must keep the promise to my father" she replied.

She offered to give me back my hanky but I pushed it away and said, "Keep it". Further conversation was interrupted by the announcement to fasten our seatbelts. The roar of engines and prepared for takeoff. She whispered to me "This is the first time I have flown "Don't worry" I reassured her. "I have flow over 200 times its second nature to me" She seemed relieved that she was sitting next to a seasoned plane traveler, and as the plane moved forward towards the runway she grasped my hand and smiled "I hope you don't mind me holding your hand". I smiled back and clasped her hand in mine. As we raced up the runway for lift off, she squeezed my hand tightly. It was hurting but I did not restrain her, as I was in sympathy with her apprehension of her first flight.

Once the plane had reached its flight path and settled down she released my hand, and smiled at me "Thank you for being my comfort on the take-off, I hope I did not hurt you hand too much".

I shook my head to the side and pressed for more information about her intended husband. "So you say you have never the man you will marry?" "No, but I have seen a few photos of him" I shook my head. "I find that strange to marry somebody you do not know. In the west marriage is based on love, silly question I know, but do you love him after seeing his photos?" She took my hand and clasped it in her own two hands. "Can I be honest with you Dexter?" I nodded and she continued "I do not know him or if I will love him he is like a strange to me" She paused and looking into my eyes "I know you better than I do him" pausing again she asked "Are you married?" Having informed her of my marital status she then asked me a number of leading questions, "How long you been married? And you have children?" A few more questions she asked about my wife and what she was like. She was surprised that I had married an Asian girl. She then surprised me by asking "Have you ever cheater on your wife?" She gulped "I'm sorry I should not have asked you that question" I tapped her knee with my left hand. "It's ok, but would you think ill of me? I had been unfaithful." Usher put her hand on my knee and squeezed it gently." I would not change my opinion of you whatever you tell me" I found myself confessing to Usher my love for Penny and brief affairs with other ladies. She seemed excited and her hand slide inside my thigh. I then asked her

"Can I ask you something personal?" She grinned showing a set of perfectly white teeth", I can guess what you ask me. the answer is I am still a virgin".

We were in conversation for a long time and we exchanged stories of our lives before the time dictated that we should sleep. This plane was fitted which curtains so as we decided to lie back in our seats. The flight attendant pulled to curtain round. Usher was not showing any inhibition as she leaned over to my seat and let her face come directly in line with mine. She looked for some indication or rejection but when she saw that I opened my mouth she took the initiative to put her lips on mine. For a girl who claimed to be a virgin she sure knew how to kiss. She took my hand and laid it on her breast, and to encourage me more her hand was on my groin. I was putty in her hand as she unzipped my fly and released my appendage. She showed delight in its size that was fully grown. This was as close as I had ever come to being a member of the mile-high club. I could not resist her charms and my hand delved between her legs and was aware that her pubes were not shaven. She was certainly wet and mutual gratification was achieved, just as well she had tissues in her handbag.

She still insisted she was a virgin, but only that she had never been penetrated. Two ex-boyfriends she had been in liaison with had showed her the delights of mutual masturbation, being from a strict Hindu family any relationship of a romantic nature was forbidden. As far as her parents were concerned she had never had a boyfriend. We fell asleep, cuddled up close together my zip done up but her upper body was exposing her breasts and she bad me hold them as we slept. I often used to wonder why the first woman was called Eve, was it because she was the root of evil? After all it was she that tempted Adam the man, and ever since then, women have tempted men and I don't think the majority of men would decline a portion of sex if it were offered.

Chapter 20

USHER AND I WERE IN ADJACENT ROOMS

Once the plane touched down at New Delhi airport it was a long journey by train to where I would be working. I said goodbye to Usher and headed for the train. I found my compartment and had just settled down when I looked up to see Usher standing there. To cut a long story short, she was going to the village next to where I would be staying. My mind drifted back to the time 1 met Penny on the train to Wick. On this occasion there were too many people in this carriage. We could not be too close as on the plane but we were talking as much as we could. The train journey took us two hour and meant that we had to join another train for the next stage of the journey. Unfortunately, the train we should have connected with had broken down and had to wait for it to be repaired. This situation resulted in an overnight stay in this small town with only a single hotel able to accommodate the train passengers. Was it a coincidence that Usher and I were in adjacent rooms?

I took her cases to her room and was just about to leave and go to my room when she pulled me to body and started to kiss me. "Come back after you put your cases in you room". How could 1 refuse. I knocked on the door and she greeted me dressed in just a towel. "Come in Dexter" she indicated with her arm. She pointed towards the bed and licking her lips she announced, "I have never been naked with a man who is naked and laid together, so before I marry I want you to teach me what I should do". Usher let her towel fall to the floor and my eyes feasted upon her pure beauty. Her skin brown and flawless. Her body was perfect with neat pointed breasts and nipples dark and protruding. She mentioned to me to come close to her. As I stood there, she placed her hands on the buttons of my shirt slowly undoing them until the last button and then withdrawing my shirt tail from my trousers and sliding it off my torso. She licked the hairs on my chest at the same time undid my trouser belt and unfastened the top button before unzipping me and letting my trousers fall on the ground. I stepped out of them and stood before her in just my Y fronts. She stood back opened her hands wide and with caution slipped her thumbs into the waistband. Kneeling before me methodically sliding them down to my knees. Her eyes lit up as my organ swung out and brushed against her mouth. My pants just above my knees, she manipulated my sex in both hands looked up into my eyes and whispered "I have taken one in my mouth, but if you let me I will take yours" I never said a word but held it to her mouth and watch as she engulfed it.

We slept together and I did everything other than penetration. I told her "That is for your new husband, and I don't think he would want damaged goods". Usher kissed me full on the lips and whispered "did I tell you he is 82 years of age and I don't think he will want to do it, that's why I want you to give me yours as a wedding present". I did refuse but in the other ways, I satisfied her. I do not think she was too disappointed. Sleep overcame us after a long period of intense foreplay.

In the morning we had to be up early and board the train for the last leg of the journey. It was very hot, so wearing shorts was the order of the day. Usher wore another sari. I had to admire her beauty in that traditional attire. So she was to be married to a bloke of 82. I felt certain that if he made love to her once in the manner she required he would not live to do it again. She, I seemed certain would love him to death literally.

She and I alighted from the train at the same station. Three Indian gentlemen in traditional costume met her and escorted her to a waiting cart that was harnessed to a cow. As for myself a jeep vehicle was waiting for me and the Indian driver took my cases and put them in the back of the vehicle and we drove off along the track an excuse for a road. He told me that he had been waiting for the train since yesterday. I explained about the delay but he apparently was aware of it and the camp commandant told him to stay overnight and meet me when the train got in whatever time it was.

The journey to the camp took four hours over mostly rough terrain, unmade roads full of potholes and dead animals. My body was so sore when we got to the camp that after a quick meeting with the commandant and I was shown to my cabin by a young Indian boy to deep inside the camp perimeter. Basic ablutions awaited me, external toilet where one stood up to do numbers twos, as well as number ones. The shower was reminiscent of the type in Africa, but outside with just a canvas covering. Pump action to force the water up, and of course cold water. My cabin was not dissimilar to the one in Africa a bed, cupboard, chest of a draws a table and chair. Unlike my bed in Africa that was a double on legs this one was a single on the floor. Dimensions of this cabin barely the the size of a prison cell ten-foot square. Before anything else. I took a shower, then surveyed this mountainous region on the Pakistan Indian border.

The only incident that comes to mind in this territory was a serious case of slavery. This was on my first of three monthly assignments to India. My houseboy had just finished cleaning my cabin when I got a hand delivered message from the runner of one of my informers. It told of some unusual activity a mile from the camp, I went to my jeep and with the company of the runner; we drove to the place that was identified in the message.

From and observation point behind some rocks and under cover of darkness, we observed four Asian men leading a number of girls to a wailing truck. We had seen an Arabic looking guy putting a fist full of rupees into the hands of four guys, they walked away and the Arab was joined by two other Asian guys who lifted the children into the truck. My informer crept up behind me without warning I turned to face him and only the sight of his face prevented me from lashing out with my fists. The action was about to materialize when four police vehicles arrived on the scene and we watched as the police opened fire on the kidnappers and the other Asians, who were busy sharing out their proceeds from the sale of the girls. After the Arab was shot and one other guy, the others surrendered to the police. The treatment they obtained from the police was a lot worse than had they been killed. The police had no sympathy for these kidnappers and I saw two of them having their hands chopped off and another his leg was amputated by a saw. I heard their screams as they penetrated the air.

After some loud voices and accusations from the police one of the Asians was decapitated. This scene of carnage turned my stomach over. I watched as the police opened the back of the truck and released the children who quickly departed this area of slaughter. The police then got back in their vehicles and drove away When it was safe to do so we emerged from behind the rocks and I took several photographs. Using the lights of my jeep to show the victims clearly and to enable me to get come clear pictures.

These pictures were to be seen in many newspaper, TV, and newsreels around the world. The outcry from the world press was mixed. Most papers in the West condoned this act as barbaric Police brutality and a disgrace to law enforcement officers in India. In the Middle East and parts of Asia, an alternative viewpoint. Saying it was a justifiable punishment and retribution for the abuse of young girls. I wat not aware if the police who were instrumental in this butchery were ever reprimanded. Following my expose' of this incident. The UN pulled me out of that camp in India by helicopter.

This incident happened just 8 days before I was due to return to England anyway. The reason for my instant removal from the camp was that other members of the slave gang who had survived might have targeted me. My name and photo was attributed to the story and the photos taken. This was an inadvertent mistake, since the UN information office only wanted the story and pictures to be assigned to a member of or UN force information office in India not to a named individual

I flew home to be with my Family minus Linda who was still in the states. I did not have to tell her about the incident in India, as it was in all the newspapers. Other journalist, in the media all wanted me to expand upon my experience. I was instructed by the UN information Office not to say anything in respect of the incident. All I was to say was "No comment". The Herald wanted my son to get an exclusive interview with me on the action but I had to decline. However, I did give my boy an interview on the subtler side of my experiences in India.

I was recalled to UN HQ in NY for a debriefing. It was godsend since that is where Linda and Penny were filming. No time for any real extra marital relations with Penny as Von came with me. I did manage to obtain an hour with Penny away from the main part of NY and we met in Greenwich Village at a restaurant. We talked, held hands and shared a passionate kiss before we both had to get back to our respective appointments.

My officer gave me two days off after the debriefing it was a great opportunity to be with our daughter. Linda took us to many places of interest including Times Square, The Empire State building, The Statue of Liberty Central Park etc. *(New York City, arguably the world's most vibrant and sprawling metropolis, occupies five boroughs, each with its own distinct identity. After all, before his historic 1898 consolidation, Manhattan, Brooklyn, the Bronx, Queen and Saten Island were each independent municipalities. Manhattan, home of the most recognizable sites, Central Park fly into New York over the stretch of Manhattan, one of the most stunning visuals in the 843-acre carpet of green that makes up this stunning park. Located smack-dab in the middle of the borough).*

Von flew back to the UK and I was back out to India but to a different camp but still on the India side of the border with Pakistan. For security reason I was given a new identity with the name Paul Halstead. A wig with the beard and mustache home grown completed my new persona. With the wig on it seemed to completely change my character and when I met an old colleague at the airport he never recognized me. My old air force buddy Francs (Frank) Mason. Having seen him move away from the booking desk I walked up to him and tapped his shoulder. He looked round directly into my face "Yes who you want?" he asked. I smirked and in an accent retorted You FM that being his nickname. He pulled back from my face and glared at me "Do I know you?" He continued. I moved my face closer he retreated aback and exclaimed "I don't know who you are and I'm not in the habit of kissing men" I laughed. "Take a closer look FM you do know me". He stared at me, precariously, before exclaiming "Bloody Hell Dexter, you have changed how did you restore your hair, last time I saw you, you had short hair and slightly receding, and what goes with the face furniture. I explained to him the reason why and we spent time speaking over old times and in particular his and my arrest in Pretoria a few back.

In all I spent 8 more assignments in India and managed not to be involved in any scandal or incidents of life risking situations. I was even avowing being hunted by women. Well not quite. Two years after my first UN assignment in India, I met up with Usher again. It was May 1976. I was in the departure lounge to Bombay (Mumbai) airport. I was sitting reading a trashy novel; my legs were akimbo, my head buried in the book. Clean shaven now and the wig no more as the publicity over the kidnapping incident was long forgotten. I looked up to see a pair of long brown legs and above a slim skirt above the knees, raising my head slightly and her face came into view. She sat down next to me then gently pulled on my ear "Do you remember me Mr. Dexter

Barren "She whispered. I stifled a laugh and grimaced "How can one forget such a beauty as you Usher?" She leaned over and kissed me on the cheek.

"So how is your octogenarian husband?" I enquired "He is dead" she grunted. "I am a young widow" So! I continued "when did this happen?" "last week, and all I want to do is get out of this God forsaken country and get back to England." She concluded. She offered me a cigarette I and took my pipe out of my pocket and after lighting her cancer stick lit my pipe blowing the smoke away from her face. Usher continued to explain her new circumstances.

"My Hushed died of natural causes. His personal valet told me that he died during the night. It was not the type marriage I was hippy in. He only wanted me as a trophy bride. I never slept with him or he see me naked and certainly

I did not see him with nothing on, but he was kind to me I suppose I never wanted for anything except sex and I was not able to get that from anybody. I was always being watched by one of his servant or bodyguards, I never left his palace unless one of his bodyguards came with me. I did like one of them but too soon and in time I found out he was gay. You know I have not had sex with anybody since you obliged me 2 years ago". After this outpouring in which remarkably she never stopped for breath she looked at me with those brown eyes trying to mesmerize me. "So you must be quite rich now Usher" I exclaimed. Her reply was interrupted by the airport announcement. "BOAC Flight 675 from Bombay to London has been cancelled until 8 am tomorrow morning." Usher looked at me with her mouth agape. "Guess we will have to spend the night in the hotel."

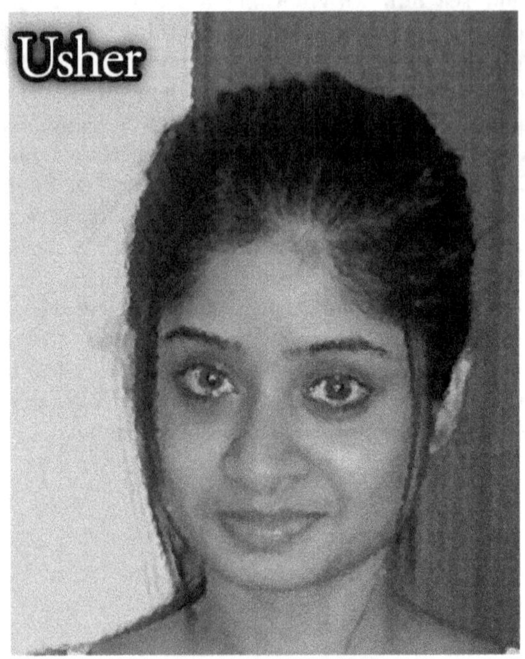

Chapter 21

UNDER HER SPELL

I was under her spell as she laid her Amex card on the reception desk and demanded "I want the best suite in this" The receptionist took the card entered the details and called a page boy to take our cases to the suite. After giving the boy a rupee note, she waited for him to leave the room before she turned to me and melted her lips against mine. As she pulled back, I noticed that she had undone my top button, and was slipping out of her dress. There were no words spoken. I did try but she pressed her finger against my lip. As she stepped out her dress to stand before me in her pastel underwear she moved in towards me and pulling my belt through the loops of my trousers they automatically fell down. I stepped out of my trousers after releasing my shoes from my feet. My shirt was fully unbuttoned and removed by Usher then pushed me towards the large king size bed.

I was on my back and she lay across my chest twiddling with my chest chairs, her hand later traversing from my chest down to my navel, but not under my underpants. She then took pleasure in licking my nipples. Eventually, she turned her attention to my face where her tongue went into my ears, along the bridge of my nose, on my eyelids before her lips met mine and with her tongue forced my mouth open. She was on top of me pushing her knee into my groin as with her hands she was holding my head covering my ears. The movement of her body was arousing me. She was content just to gyrate against my body. This foreplay was to last for an undetermined time and each time I went to talk, her mouth covered mine.

Eventually I had to visit the bathroom so I maneuvered her body from off mine to my side and whispered "I must relieve myself Usher". She lay there and watched my departure into the bathroom. I stood over the toilet bowl, removing as I did my y fronts and began to empty my bladder. Usher moved in behind me her hand then directed the flow of my urine in the WC. Having then completed my ablutions, she turned me round to face her. It was then that I noticed she had removed her underwear and all she was wearing were her long earring and the familiar red marking on her forehead. She was content just to hold me in that position with her hands clasped round my head, her mouth was on mine using her tongue to force my lips to open. My sex was brushing against her now shaved pubes. She made no further attempt to manipulate it. She was happy just to hold me having been starved of affection for over two years.

In time we were back into the bedroom and under the sheets she continued to run her hands over my body giving each part equal attention. I reciprocated and found my touch on her body felt so much of stimulation. She leaned over to me yet again and kissed me gently, but no forcing of my lips to apart. She spoke

"You know Dexter, I was so desperate for affection since my deprivation of any physical contact with my late husband" I smiled "I can understand that a woman just as a man has needs" She ran her hand over my cheek and looked into my eyes into her mouth only inches from mine. Again she spoke "You know I am now a very rich woman, my late husband's four sons wanted me to leave the palace, we lived in and as a settlement, they gave me 10 million rupees, there was no way I would inherit all his fortune due to a prenuptial agreement which I had to sign" again I smiled "So with that amount of money you will never want for anything in your life again" she touched my lips with her two fingers and continued "The only thing it can't buy is real love, I love you will all my heart and soul Dexter and I always will and I prayed we could meet again even though I know you are married so I cannot have you all to myself but if I could be with you sometimes will be my greatest desire" she paused. "Is that possible?" I licked my lips before I kissed her "It is possible I could accommodate you if that is what you want, but you must understand I will not leave my wife or my mistress" Perhaps her smile was forced but replied "yes that is ok for me as long as we can spend time together and it is you and only you who will eventually undo my virginity". The remainder of the night we slept with our bodies entwined but before our slumber we helped each other to climax by hands and mouths, but no penetration.

We went back to the airport and we sat next to each other on the flight back to the UK. Usher accepted my polite request "My wife is meeting me at the airport so please do not be by my side when we go through the customs shed". She smiled and slipped me a piece of paper with her new address and phone number. She went through the customs on her own and once she was cleared I came through myself and outside in the man hall, Von met me and we went home. Deprived on affection for the last month we wasted no time in sharing our bodies in bed.

More assignments on behalf of the UN took me through to a three-year employment under their auspices. Usher never found anybody that she could write with, and I saw her a few more times as with Penny. I was finally to penetrate

Usher on our 7th meeting. I went up to Leeds and she met me at the station. She drove me home in her car. The house was on the outskirts of the city, not far from where she owned one of her six boutiques. She had obviously put her money to good use me. She confided in me that she had dates two men one Indian and one Englishman but after the first date she could not continue. Her reason was simple she could not feel for them the way she felt for me. I was given a guided tour of her 4-bedroom house. She at times had her brother and his wife come to stay. It was sad he was brain damaged after the accident that derived Usher of her parents, but credit her sister in law she stood by him.

We sat and talked for a while, as it had been 2 months since we last met. She took initial pleasure in just holding my hands and slipping me the occasional kiss as we conversed. After two cups of tea and a slice of cake Usher took my hand and uttered, "shall we go to bed". Like a child crossing the threshold I was led upstairs to her bedroom. She released my hand and undid a draw in her beside cupboard and took out a packet of three. "I think you should use these as I am ready for you to seduce me and I want to feel you inside me now. A big grin on her face this was the day she would lose her virginity.

We watched each other undress and I was pleased to see that her pubic hair was now looking more appetizing than it had before. After returning to the UK she had decided to let her hair grow as I told her I preferred hair to baldness. We slipped between she sheets and began our foreplay lots of mouth to mouth and she took delight in running her tongue up my hairy chest biting gently on my nipples as she lay above me. I managed to grasp her breasts and with my thumbs rubbed her ripples until they became hard. She was now sitting aside me on my lap and her hand was gently massaging my sex. To a size that would be satisfactory for her. Leaning over to the cable cupboard she took a condom out of the packet. At first she looked confused as to what to do with it. I took it from her and slipped it over the top and she pulled it down so it was fitting properly. Her breathing was deep, and between breaths she stuttered "Dexter be careful please don't hurt me, be gently. My condom fitted organ was at her opening and slowly I let it enter. At first it caused her to shout out ah! But then it was all the way in and I pumped as Usher's body shook and she was throwing her face side to side. "I love it I love it" she shouted "fuck me harder Dexter fuck me hard, I want to come" It was not long before I filled the condom and I could see the pleasure written on Usher's face as the climaxed with me. Evidence as if needed that she was a virgin lay on the bed sheet. I left her lying on the bed as I went into the bathroom to remove the condom. On my return, she got up from the bed and hugged me whispering many times "Thank you Dexter thank you Dexter, you really made me feel good. I love you so much".

I left Usher in a very happy mood and promised that I would see her again is 5 weeks in Leeds. I was very careful in my three relationships over the next few years. Von did not know about my modal relationship with either Penny or Usher and Penny did not know about Usher. I was to see more of Usher in 1976 when being back with ONMA they asked me to cover the reporter in the North East of England. I was based in Leeds for 4 weeks. I was in Usher's bed every night accepting for 6 nights when I went home to Elstree to be with Von and my family. My son was now working for the Daily Mail and Linda was appearing in a number of films on TV.

The posting I had contemplated but would never realize would ever be was to spend one month in the Philippines in 1979. It was to be a family affair as both Linda and my son Dexter had obtained time off to come with me Von and her mother to visit the country in which I had spent 3 years as a child. It would be a a wonderful opportunity for the family to meet relatives they had never met. It was a long flight and we were tired after being in the air for 23 hours. We arrived at Manila late at night after two spots in Singapore and

Sydney. We went to our hotel just outside the capital and so tired we all went to bed as quickly as we could.

The City of Manila (Tagalog: Lungsod ng Maynila), or simply Manila or Maynila, is the capital of the Philippines and one of

the 17 cities and municipalities that make up Metro Manila. It is located on the eastern sores of Manila Bay, on the western portion of the National Capital Region, in the western side of Luzon. Manila is one of the central hubs of a thriving metropolitan area home to over 19 million people. As of 2009, Manila ranks as the world's eleventh largest metropolitan area and the fifth largest urban area by population. Manila is also ranked as one of the most densely populated cities in the world. The city has over 100 parks throughout the city.) We stayed in the Swagman Hotel located in the heart of this city, and walking distance from the Australian and British Embassy and within 5 miles from the airport. In the morning, the rest of the family without myself were going to Davao from where Connie, Von's mother had been born. I said goodbye to my family at the airport and catching another taxi back to the city I reported for my assignment to the Australian embassy. I was not the only POME slang for an Englishman and meaning **Prisoner of Mother England.** The other English people there were Fiona Watson working on special ops and Bob Wilson who I understand was dealing with something to do with diversity.

I spent a day wandering round the streets of Manila in the company of Wilfred my guide; It was much like India, Brazil and Africa where a large majority of kids were begging on the streets. In my caring generosity, I empty my pockets of pesos at several of the street camps, despite Wilfred telling me not to. I could understand why as we were then pursued by several kids and had to grab a taxi to be free of them.

Parts of Manila were not unlike other cities I had visited, but fewer vehicles on the road than in London. *(It was not hard to realize that this country was one of the most prosperous after the war but their head of state President Ferdinand Marcos was a corrupt dictator of who declared martial law in 1972. Because of close ties between United States and President Marcos, the U.S. governmenkt continued to support Marcos even though his administration was well-known for massive corruption and extensive human rights abuse.)*

Part of my task in the Philippines was to discover just how corruption was affecting life in this beautiful country. I felt sorry for the high percentage of people who had no jobs, it was high 60 percent or more. I was not impressed when Wilfred managed to obtain permission for me to visit a jail. I was horrified to see that male children and adults shared the same cells. I was to learn to my disgust that many of these children suffered abuse at the hands of perverted males. The prison authorities were powerless to do anything to prevent it. It was my general opinion of the Philippines that I liked their respect for people, and noticed how they appreciated the older members of their community. Sadly, this is lacking in the UK where I have found most aggressive attitudes towards older people from some youngsters. Thankfully, those that have had good parents who instructed them in discipline did have respect for their elders.

When my family reached Davao in Mindanao in the South of the Philippines, Von phoned me to say they arrived safely and were due to meet some of her relatives later that day. In the second week, I was there, I managed to obtain time off for three days to fly down to Davao and meet my family who were staying in the *(Waterfront Hotel. Nestled along the picturesque Davao Gulf, its open air corridors provide a refreshing view of the hotel's beautifully landscaped tropical green and the scenic view of the Davao Gulf. Suites and guest room which tastefully done interiors and equipped with luxurious amenities. The rooms overlook pristine white sand beaches across Samal Island, the swimming pool amidst lush gardens and towering coconut, which provide coconut wine. Aside from the swimming pool, resort facilities include majestic conference rooms, 6 different restaurants to satisfy even the most discriminating taste, and a weaving center. Room service offers a wide selection of Asian, Western and Filipino Favourites.)*

(The City of Davao (Tagalog Lungsod ng Davaw; is the largest city located on the Island of Mindanao. It is also one of the most progressive cities. With its international airport and seaports being among the busiest cargo handlers in the southern part of the Philippines. Davao City is also one of several cities in the Philippines that are independent of the Mindanao province. The city is the regional center for Davao Region. Population in 2007 was estimated to be 1,363,330. Davao City is the business, investment and tourism center for southern Philippines. The city has many of the fines beaches and

mountain resorts in the country as well as its highest peak, Mount Apo.) Trying to get used to the heat was a task in itself as every day the thermometer was 30 or more. Von was pleased to see me and we spent most of the day meeting relatives that were not even born when Connie left the Philippines. My son had taken a shine to one of his cousins it was Connie's cousins' daughter. She was 18 and he was 21. He had been with a few girlfriends more than I had before I married his mother. It was obvious that he was besotted with her. He and she reminded me of when I was young courting his mother. Aqyza my son still had the Philippines look and colour about him though his facial attributes did contain some of my genes. On the other hand, Linda took after her mother but a slightly lighter colour but could still be considered as a native of the Philippines. I was the odd one out with my lighter colour and Anglo Saxon appearance. Linda already had a boyfriend back in the UK and had no intentions of finding a Filipino boy. She was phoning him every night adding to my eventual bill for their stay in this hotel.

Chapter 22

I WENT TO THE MORGUE AND I IDENTIFIED THE BODY

My short stay was soon over and I returned to Manila to continue my duty as press officer at the Australian embassy. I was not surprised to get a phone call from Penny but was surprised to learn that she was coming to the Philippines for three days to complete a film called *'The Souther Jewel'*. We arranged to meet at a rendezvous outside of city. I waited in this restaurant at the pre-arranged time but after half an hour I became anxious. Three girls had propositioned me. I declined, I had never been with a prostitute and certainly was not about to even if Penny did not show up. I needed to use the facilities so I left the table and entered the restaurant and was shown where the toilet was, I came out just as Penny was standing outside the café and seeing I was not there was about to walk away, I called after her. She turned and ran back to me and we shared a brief kiss before we sat down and I enjoyed another beer, whilst she had a glass of white wine. We had so much to talk about, but she was anxious to be alone with me away from prying eyes. It was as well she was not wearing her dark wig, which she always wore in her films. Keeping her identity separate was always in her mind. Nobody recognized her even though a few of her films had been shown in Philippine cinemas.

We found a little hotel just around the corner from the café, I booked us in, but though asked for my passport I said I had left it in the Australian embassy. At first the clerk was not going to let us have a room but a few pesos extra and he changed his tune and we booked in under an assumed name. It was a simple room unlike my own hotel room in the Swagman hotel. We soon parted with our clothes and lay on the bed feeling each other's body. It had been a month since we last shared our bodies and both of us were anxious to make amends for this lack of carnal activity. Penny shifted her body onto mine and after rubbing her hands over my chest slipped her hand down to my sex and fed it as it was au- natural into her waiting orifice. Within a few minutes we had both climaxed and then we just rested side by side on the bed. We had booked for the night, so we wanted to make the most of it. It was more pleasure as we abandoned all inhibitions to satisfy our animal lusts. I had informed the embassy that I was not going to be in the Swagman hotel that night but would be back in the embassy in the morning. It was no concern to them of what I did with my private life and they respected it.

Three days before I was due to return with my family to the UK, I received a distressing call from my son. Von had gone out on a ferry with one of her cousins to visit another cousin on Samal Island. This small ferry she was on had been struck by a tanker. She had gone only with her cousin, as her mother Connie was not feeling well and decided to stay in the waterfront hotel. I was beside myself with grief as of the bodies recovered from the water one was identified as Von. My whole life was coming crashing down. I was given compassionate leave by the Embassy, and got the first flight to Davao. I was full of worry; my heart was pounding ad the flight did me no favours as we ran into some turbulence.

My son met me at the airport. He was trying to stop his tears as he related to me what was happening "I went to the morgue and I identified the body" he could not control the tears and continued whilst sobbing, "but dad she was so badly cut up that it was hard to realize it was mum there, the face" he paused "You would not recognize her". I held my son as close to me as I could. I had to force myself to visit the morgue. I did not want to believe that my darling wife was dead. Just one glance at her body so badly mutilated, but I had to accept it was she that laid there, the dress she wore was the one she had worn when she got on the ferry. Nothing else was there to satisfy me one way or the other her legs were sliced and part of both her arms were missing. It seemed that when the oil tanked smashed into the ferry, the tanker's propeller had churned up the bodies.

We buried the remains of both Von and her cousin in Davao and with sadness I returned home. I was given compassionate leave for one month. I phoned Penny in the USA to tell of my grief and she told me she would be straight over as a family friend. She could only stay for 2 days as she was on schedule to be on the film set for the film *'Blades of Oregon'*. Linda was filming in East Ender's in the BBC studio in Elstree. My son Aqyza was in regular communication with his Filipino girlfriend Violet, and had decided that he wanted to marry her and she was coming to England before my compassionate leave expire. He had asked me if it was all right being the circumstance of his mother's demise. I assured him "life must go on its hard I know but your happiness now is foremost in my mind now".

Penny arrived two days later and she could see me how sad I was, but with her in my house I was feeling less distraught. We were alone in the house and Penny put her arms around me and could feel how uptight I was she told me to sit in the chair and massage my neck. We were not to be alone for long hardly a kiss of affection before I could hear my son's car pulling into the drive. He had collected Linda from the studio and when they saw Penny, they seemed to be relieved that as a family friend she was here. Penny and I were not to be alone until the following morning when both my offspring had to attend to their vacations. Not to show too much haste, Penny slept in the spare room, which over the years had become her room as she always stayed with us when filming at the Elstree studios. After the family had left, I had a visit from Penny, she was wearing a very short nightdress. She smiled at me "move over darling" I stopped her "It's too soon Penny, but give me time I am still grieving". She sat on the bed, put her arm round me and held my hand. She kissed me and it felt good. Not in this bed Penny, this was where Von and myself slept for 21 years. I got out of the bed still in my nude state, as I had always slept and whispered, "If you want to give me comfort lets go to your bed." I took her hand and led her back to her room.

I got into her bed first and she took off her nightdress and joined me. It was not for sex but just to feel the comfort of a warm body next to mine. We both fell asleep only to be woken by the sound of somebody downstairs. I went to my own rom and quickly pulled on a pair of trousers and a shirt. I knew who was downstairs, it was Connie, Von's mother. Penny came down fully dressed a few minutes later. I was in the lounge wading through some paperwork and I overheard Connie say to Penny "we are so grateful you came over for the family, they need a friend now after what happened to my daughter. Dexter, my son-in-law is so down. I don't know how he can cope, but I know you will help us all come to terms with this tragedy".

I had just celebrated my 40th birthday, I had paid a visit to Usher in Leeds and she made a proposition to me "Dexter, how about you and I in time getting married?" I was a little taken aback by this request but I still responded in an ambiguous manner "it's too soon yet Usher, give me time, it has only been 4 months since Von was killed. Let me think about it in 6 months". She put her arms round me and pressed her lips against mine then whispered "I will marry you if you want me too, do you like that" I have a forced grin shook my head and exclaimed "Give me time Usher, it's far too soon, and anyway I have my mistress to consider too." Usher stood up and glared at me in a hurt manner "But who do you love the most, me or her?" Again a force smile "I have to be honest, I love you both equally and don't force me to make a choice, if I could marry you both I would" Usher sighed and putting her arms round me kissed me full on my mouth. Nibbling on my ear she again whispered "If you marry her, you can still see me as you can see me as often as you can, I am not the jealous type, if I can't have all of you, I am willing to settle for half or a quarter whatever so long as I can be part of your life" she paused. "Can you at least promise me that Dexter" her arms now in a full embrace and her lips lingering close to my lips. "You have my word on that Usher, after 5 years of friendship I don't want to lose you" I informed her.

It was February 1980 and I was home on leave from a month in Russia, glad to come back to a warmer climate. Temperatures of minus 20 below and the only time I did not sleep naked. The heating in none of the 4 Hotels I stayed in could not satisfy what my bodily requirements. Penny was still in the states but would be home 2 days after me. She was a regular visitor to our home and both my offspring indicated in a roundabout sort of way that I should marry her. Violet my son's girlfriend was enjoying being in England with him and he had proposed to her. A day for the wedding had been set for the same day as his birthday in February. I would be home for that day as my agency was sending me to Scotland to cover for their reporter who was retiring at the age of 65. I was informed that it would be permanent if I wanted it. I asked if I could think about it and give my answer in two weeks. This was accepted.

I had a few days before I would take up my post in Scotland. I waited until Penny arrived, determined to pop the question. The hints from my family including my mother-in-law Connie made it clear in my mind that I should propose. It was 6 months now since we had laid poor Von's body in the ground and it was time I moved on. After all I had known Penny was over 10 years and had been a friend to my family for 6 years.

I greeter Penny at the door and the entire family was there. Was I going to make a fool of myself would Penny turn me down or hopefully accept. I took her hand and led her into the lounge where they were all seated. I dropped down on one knee took her hand in mine and asked the important life changing question. Penny threw her arms round me and in full view of the family kissed me and exclaimed yes Dexter Barren I will be your wife.

We were officially engaged with a small family party a few days later. To retain her identity secret, as she always wanted no mention was to be made to the press. Penny always maintained her show business life and private life would always remain separate. Wig on for films and wig off of her private life. Violet was excited as Aqyza my son for their forthcoming nuptials. She enjoyed talking to me in her native tongue, as my son was still not fluent enough although his grandmother had taught him as much as she could. Like me he often got confused with what language he was speaking in. He was fluent in Spanish and French but coming along slowly in Tagalog. In fact, it was Linda who was the more proficient speaking it even better than her French or Spanish.

I was home for the wedding and only Violet's father came

over from the Philippines. Her mother did not to travel, as she was not a well person. At least her father gave her away. My brothers and my sister came to the wedding with their offspring's all young adults. Most of my nephews and nieces were already married and had their own offspring. So, I was a great uncle at 40 as three days before my son's wedding, Derek's son's wife gave birth to a little ball called Freddy. The church we chose was the Baptist church in Borehamwood, which we as a family had adopted as our place of worship. The Elstree Lake Company held the wedding reception in their function room. Aqyza and Violet spent their honeymoon on the Island of Ibiza. It was very late when the guests all departed some going straight home whilst others were accommodated in our home or the home shared by my mother and mother-in-law. Despite our engagement, I did not share a bed with Penny whilst the family were in the hose, we would only do this once we married. The date set was for Saturday April the 5th. We both agreed on minimum fuss and only a small quiet service and reception at our house. Penny wanted no publicity. We kept the guests to just my brothers and sister and their spouses. Our mothers and of course my children. My son Aqyza did the honour of giving Penny away. We spent our honeymoon quietly in a little fishing village in Devon.

It was a quaint little cottage we had rented for 1 week only as I had to be up in Scotland to perform my duties as the agency correspondent. I had agreed to cover this post for 4 months. This would take me through to the end of June 1980. I shared the driving with Penny and we stopped on route in Bournemouth so I could show her where Von and I spent our Honeymoon. Alas that hotel was no more and replaced by the Round House.

We were tired when we got to the cottage but not too tired to consummate our marriage legally. I felt there was more abandonment from Penny, as this was a legal situation and no more mistress but wife. It was so isolated that in the morning, we went skinny-dipping and for the first time in our lives we made love outside on a secluded section of the beach and then cleaned ourselves off in the water.

We knew that our different vocations would see us more apart than together. However, although I would be in Scotland based in Edinburgh until the end of June. Penny was filming in close by Glasgow. For 5 weeks from mid-May until the end of June. We would be able to see a lot of each other. Edinburgh was not too far from Glasgow just under 50 miles. We rented a small house in Bathgate 30 miles from Glasgow. Before that however, Penny had to return to the States to finish filming *"Sands of Chance"* in Hollywood. Long lingering kisses, as I left her at the airport for her flight to the states and I went to the other terminal for my flight to Edinburgh.

Chapter 23

IT WAS AN OPEN MARRIAGE

It was lonely in that house in Bathgate it was off the beaten track nearest neighbor was 1 mile away. I would be there on my own for four weeks before Penny could join me. I phoned Usher from the Bathgate house, I already told her that I was getting married to Penny; I know she was upset because she sounded disappointed and ended the conversation almost immediately. I had not spoken to her since the 4th of April now, 10 days later I was phoning her. Hello sweetness Dexter here" I exclaimed. There was a pregnant pause before she answered. "I was so upset when you phone me to say you were getting married to my rival, but the deed is done now, and so long as you keep your promise to let me have some of you I will be happy, so where are you now?" "In Scotland, a place called Bathgate I have rented a house here I moved from the one in Edinburgh, I did not like it there" I lied as the only reason I moved was so that Penny and I could spend every night together when she came to Glasgow for her film.

"How far is Bathgate Dexter? I can come up there for a couple of days if you let me and want me as much as I want you" Usher responded without a pause. "It's just over 200 miles according to my AA map four and half hours driving or by train it will take you 3 hours" I informed her. "Fine, can you tolerate me for 4 nights?" was her instant reply. "I would love to have you for four nights" I chuckled. Usher wasted no time and the following day I got a page bleep to go to the nearest phone. It was Usher, she was at the Station and wanted me to collect her. I had to finish my business in Glasglow police station and told her I could be there in half an hour and to take herself off to the café opposite the station and I would meet her there. Lucky, I never got a speeding ticket as it only took me 10 minutes on the motorway. A kiss was my greeting and as she happily always did for the last 6 years nibbled me on my ear. We were only 10 minutes' drive from the station, 15 minutes after leaving the station we were getting undressed to get into bed. It had been three weeks since I had last seen Usher and she was more eager for carnal activity than I was. So married only a few weeks and here I was having it off with my only mistress now since Penny was now my wife. Life would be easier now with only 2 women to alternate with. Penny of course did not know about Usher. She was quite prepared for me to have sex with whomever I wanted so long as it was not prostitutes and I took precautions. Penny had informed me a long time ago that she had casual sex but not long term and caution was her middle name. She asked me during our honeymoon if I would be upset if she carried on with casual sex with other men, or should she stop. I responded to her that it was her choice, her body and so long as she still loved me it was not a problem. What they call an open marriage.

Usher had been reading the Kama Sutra the Indian book on sexual practice and positions. Eager to try out as many as she could the next 4 nights and days when we could be devoted to the art of seduction. Worry about making her pregnant had been eradicated as Usher was using a IUD, Intra Uterine Device like that fitted inside her womb that prevented my sperm reaching her eggs. Usher was only 25 to my 40 but that age gap existed between my late father and mother, so no problem to me. It was quite an education and excited to try out so many ways to seduce my lover. *(The Kama sutra is an ancient Indian text accepted to be the customary work on human sexual behavior in Sanskrit literature compiled by the Indian scholar Mallanaga Vatsayana. The manuscript consists of practical advice on sex mostly in text, with a large amount of poetry. Kama means sensual or sexual pleasure, and sutra means the thread that binds the effects together, refer to a cliché or a collection in the form of a manual. The modern English word suture is derived from the same root.)*

Mostly I was working from home with visits to police stations in Edinburgh, Glasgow and surrounding towns to obtain information about incidents. Sometimes, I had to go to Aberdeen Dundee, Perth, Ayr, Kilmarnock etc. Most of the big stories worth publishing abroad came from the major cities. I got a call on the third day of Usher being at the house calling to an incident that was underway in Glasgow near the docks. I was there inside 30 minutes and was watching three men all with swords holding a three people hostage.

The swords poised round the necks of two young women and a young man. The police were present with a large contingent trying to negotiate the release of the captives. Several armed officers were in strategic positions. The three hostage holders were out in the open in a demolition sight. The area had been cleared for the construction of new offices and plant. Looking through binoculars, I was able to identify the three assailants as white and of Eastern European descent. I made out a few words of Russian. With this information, I provided to the police they were able to locate a fluent Russian linguist to come to the scene. Despite the presence of the linguist, the Russians would not release their captives unless a Russian sailor in police custody was released. This was not possible since the Russian sailor they were holding had brutally hacked a prostitute to death with an axe. The police were slowly losing patience. It was agreed that the only way to end this standoff was to eliminate all three men at once. Three trained marksmen had to fire into the heads of all three captors at exactly the same time precisely. It had to be that way without any hesitation. Watches synchronized. The police made one final request for them to put down their swords. They made no response other than restating their former demand that the sailor be released. The signal was made and at the precise second three shots rang out and the three assailants feel to the ground dead. Neither of the hostages was harmed.

It was the very first time I was being filmed talking about an incident and within a few minutes my broadcast was being shown around the world. My face and voice were being seen by billions of people in many countries. I used my linguistic talents to broadcast in French, Russian, Spanish, Chinese and German and of course English. I had to follow this up with another live broadcast 20 minutes later. Whilst I was at the chuck wagon having a mug of tea and bacon roll, a police officer asked me to bring my cameraman to the far end of the demolition sight. The sight that greeted me brought back memories of the carnage in India. Two bodies, which I assumed were female, had been butchered, heads decapitated arms and legs hacked off plus the addition of their own entails being removed and strewn over the floor. What type of person would do this? Somebody was mentally unstable?

When I got back to the house in Bathgate, Usher was curious about the incident I had attended. I only told her about the shooting nor the carnage. Turning on the TV I was surprised that it was my report that was on both Commercial TV and the BBC. Evidently the two major news companies BBC news and ITN did not cover this incident. Usher was shocked as the edited version of my account was shown. My description of the butchered bodies was also edited. My son Aqyza phoned me from home to tell me he had seen my first news broadcast. I did not feel in the mood for sex that night as the sight I had seen earlier was playing on my mind.

Usher returned to Leeds and once more I was on my own. Later that day, after Usher had been departed for all of 6 hours, I got a very disturbing phone call from my mother-in-law. "Dexter, its Connie, I am a bit disturbed. I had a phone call from somebody saying hello Mum it is Yvonne. I put the phone down and it rang again. The voice that sounded like Yvonne said I am alive; I have been suffering from amnesia. The phone then was cut off". My heart missed a beat was this really Von had she really lost her memory and so not been able to contact us. I phoned my office in Australia and told them what my mother-in-law told me. They assured me that their vast network would make some enquiries and would get back to me as soon as possible. I did not sleep that night. The phone rang at 6 am I rushed downstairs to answer it. It was Penny. When I finished telling her about what my former mother-in-law had said, there was silence from Penny before she responded. "If it is true and she is still alive, I am your wife and she is your wife, this is most complicated" she paused. "Maybe it's a hoax, we will just have to wait and see".

By the time Penny, my new wife had arrived, I had not heard anymore from Connie, neither from ONMA who said they would investigate. I was not in the mood for total sex suffices to say just a hug and kiss would be sufficient. Penny understood what I was going through. The very thought that Von might still be alive almost nine months after we buried a body that we identified as my late first wife. My son, Aqyza phoned me "Dad, I have received a letter here addressed to you and it is I am sure in Mum's handwriting". My heart missed several beats, I was dumbstruck to reply straight away. "Dad you still there?" Aqyza asked. "OK Aqyza" I responded. "Open it and read it to me".

VON'S LETTTER

My dear Dexter, it seems I have been in a strange world of not knowing who I am. It was not until I saw you on TV that I realized that I knew you, I did not fully understand how I knew you until a few days later. I tried to phone you and then phone my mother. She put the phone down on me on the two times I phoned. I write this letter in the hope that you get it. I was on the boat going to Samal Island when the ferry struck something and I was thrown out of the boat. I do not remember anything else, as I must have passed out.

When I awoke, I was on beach and this man and his wife took me to their home. Later, I was taken to the Christian mission and cared for by the pastor and his wife. I could not remember anything of my past life. Slowly it is all coming back to me, I could not believe that for 9 months, I had no knowledge of who I was. However, I do now and I enclose a recent photo of me taken at the mission and the date so you will know it is me. I want to come home back to you, my mother and my loving children, Aqyza and Linda. *(The letter contained some personal stuff that convinced me without doubt that it was my wife Von.)*

BACK TO MY STORY

I phoned my office in Australia straight away and they told me they would make all the arrangements to bring my wife back to the UK. I caught the first train back to my home and both Penny and I were in a state of shock. Circumstances that was unique. My dead wife now alive and me married to Penny. What was the legal situation? It was going to take some lawyer to sort out this problem, because it was not to be taken lightly. In British law, a man cannot have two wives. Would I have to divorce Penny and remarry Von? Or would this mean I was still married to Von and the marriage to Penny was bigamy.

Von arrived back home 4 days after we had received the letter. I could not bring myself to go to the airport to meet her so my son Aqyza went with his wife Violet to bring her home. Penny was with me in the house. How were we going to tell Von that Penny and I were married? Would she accept it? I was pacing up and down like an expectant father at a birth of a child, impatient for her to come back home after nine long months in the Philippines. I heard the car pull up outside in the drive. I was shaking like a leaf; Connie opened the door and fell into her daughter's arms. They hugged for many minutes before Von saw me standing by Penny and then threw herself into my arms and my lips were pressed against hers. This was no hallucination this was my wife Von. My first wife I had married in 1958.

We sat down and I had to tell her that having been convinced she was dead; I took Penny as my wife. I did not know what her reaction would be to this confession. She looked at me smiled and exclaimed "So you got two wives now" she paused then continued very slowly. "Complicated but we can sort it out, at least I am back at home alive and with you all". She hugged Linda and then Penny, after which she looked directly into her eyes and exclaimed, slowly. "Whatever will be the outcome of this unique situation Penny, you will remain an integral part of this family for as long as you live".

Not the end but just the start of a new chapter in this unique situation.

Authors footnote

Although Dexter was raised as a Christian, his extra marital affairs and carnal activity with a number of different ladies is not condoned or supported by the main stream Christian Church. He was a good man at heart but his immoral lifestyle has to be addressed before he can claim to be a Christian. When a man has more than one wife he is sinning. God hates sin.

Islam has allowed a man to marry more than one wife. This has been done for the purpose of solving many social and domestic problems, which a family is confronted with from time to time. Many are the times when the general welfare of both man and woman depends upon the husband marrying another wife.

Today, the practice of plural marriage continues among tens of thousands of Mormon fundamentalists, mostly in the western United States, Canada and Mexico, where it is generally illegal. However, practitioners are almost never prosecuted unless there is evidence of abuse, statutory rape, welfare fraud, or tax evasion. Mormon fundamentalists believe that plural marriage where a man has more than one wife is a requirement for obtaining the highest "degree" within highest of three Mormon heavens.

www.ingramcontent.com/pod-product-compliance
Lightning Source LLC
Chambersburg PA
CBHW071822190726
48292CB00005B/1560